LONG ROPE

Center Point
Large Print

This Large Print Book carries the
Seal of Approval of N.A.V.H.

LONG ROPE

Dane Coolidge

CENTER POINT PUBLISHING
THORNDIKE, MAINE

This Center Point Large Print edition
is published in the year 2007 by arrangement with
Golden West Literary Agency.

The text of this Large Print edition is unabridged. In other
aspects, this book may vary from the original edition.
Printed in the United States of America.
Set in 16-point Times New Roman type.

ISBN-10: 1-60285-041-0
ISBN-13: 978-1-60285-041-5

Library of Congress Cataloging-in-Publication Data

Coolidge, Dane, 1873-1940.
Long rope / Dane Coolidge.--Center Point large print ed.
p. cm.
ISBN-13: 978-1-60285-041-5 (lib. bdg. : alk. paper)
1. Large type books. I. Title.

PS3505.O5697L66 2007
813'.52--dc22

2007013032

CONTENTS

LONG ROPE

CHAPTER I THE STRYCHNINE OUTFIT

FROM the Texas line across the Staked Plains the old Dry Trail led on—ninety miles of grass and flowers, with blossoming mesquite trees and cattle skeletons all headed west. It was May and the mockingbirds sang on the bushes; a lone horseman, well-mounted, jogged along; while before him like a beckoning finger the monument tipped the sky.

Comanche and Spaniard and many a cowman since had added his stone to that pile; until it rose, white and massive above the sea of rolling hummocks, to guide the lost wanderer in. The stakes which the early explorers had set had vanished from the Plains; but the hands of many men had reared a monument to Bottomless Spring, which had saved so many from death.

The buffalo had disappeared since Loving and Goodnight had made their first dry drive to the Pecos, and fat cattle roamed in their stead. Their right ears were swallow-forked, their left undersloped, and the old Hash-knife was burned on their hips. Mace Bowman knew the brand and the outfit well, and he knew the round-up outfit was near; but when he topped a ridge and saw the chuck-wagon below him he reined in and leaned on the horn.

A brand-new wagon with a white canvas top was parked in a little swale and about it in a circle there sat ten of the fanciest cowboys that his eyes had ever beheld. Beyond them, on the flat, a herd of cattle was being held while the ropers dragged out calves; the cook was using old-fashioned fire irons; but the boys who sat about were decked out from head to foot in the latest Rodeo finery. Their silk shirts were purple and red, their broad sombreros rich with beaver; and from hatband to spur shank, from lettered shaps to stamped leather saddle, they gleamed with hand-worked silver. He brushed away the dust from a broad plate on his own cantle and rode in, while they eyed him askance.

"Hello, boys—howdy, Cusi," he hailed. "Am I just in time, or too late?"

The cowboys nodded, still watching him intently, noting the breadth of his shoulders beneath his blue jumper, the huge coil of rope on his saddle. But only the cook made reply.

"Keep that hawse out of camp," he yapped back, petulantly; and turned back to beating his batter.

"Sure—sure," answered the cowpuncher good-naturedly; and as he reined back towards a bush the silver plate caught the sun. It is the mark in the West of a contest rider, a man who has taken first money and an ornate saddle for a prize; but they could not make out the words.

"He's a roper," muttered one as with effortless ease the stranger stepped down off his horse.

"Nope, a bronk-buster," hazarded another.

"Aw, look at that long rope!" scoffed their leader, a tall Texan with intolerant gray eyes. "Must've stole some widow-woman's clothesline. And ho-ly smoke, jest look at that saddle! Done stole that from the widow, too!"

They sat mute for a moment, every eye on the padded saddle and the huge coil of manila rope on the fork. Then a rumble of laughter swept their ranks and the stranger regarded them grimly.

"Never mind about that rope and saddle," he said. "I can rope a steer with the best of you."

"Oh, you can, hey?" spoke up the Texan. "I don't reckon you know who you're talking to. I'm Tex McMullen, the Champion Steer Roper of the World—and the Champion Bronk Rider, to boot!"

The puncher halted before him, looking him over from head to foot. Then with a scornful grunt he took a drink from the water bucket and picked up a tin plate and cup.

"I'm Mace Bowman, from Túcumcari," he answered. "The best damned cowboy in the world. I can ride any bronk that ever wore hair and beat ary one of you, roping!"

He faced them, glaring out from beneath his mane of curly hair like a buffalo bull on the prod. But no one accepted the challenge and he turned to fill up his plate.

"Jest a minute! Jest a minute!" spoke up a voice at his elbow, and the cook took the center of the stage. He was grizzled and greasy, with sourdough on his pants, a ten-days' growth of beard and a fixed, embittered smile.

"Meals are twenty-five cents," he said.

"Twenty-five cents!" repeated the puncher, incredulously. "Do you charge a cowboy? At the wagon?"

"That's what I said," snarled the cook. "And strangers pay in advance."

"You don't say!" mocked Bowman, straightening up. "So you're running a restauraw now! Well, I've rode the range since I could climb up a saddle-string but this is a new one on me. Since when did the Hashknife outfit start to charging the boys two-bits?"

"Since Colonel Breckenridge Jones done tuk over the ranch for winter headquarters for his Western Shows. My orders are—cash in advance!"

The cook struck a posture and held out one hand, but the man from Túcumcari disregarded it.

"I—I see!" he exclaimed, glancing around contemptuously at the grinning group of cowboys. "These gentlemen here are show-hands, wearing out their last year's shirts. That accounts for the shaps and the fancy spurs and the Champeen Everything of the World. Well, all I've got to say is you're a danged cheap outfit. When old John Marley was running the Hashknife a cowboy could stay all winter."

"That's right!" spoke up a sawed-off strayman who was sitting off by himself. "Come over and eat with me, Pardner, and leave them tinhorns alone. They wouldn't feed a man if he was starving."

He shoved his worn six-shooter around to the front and a silence fell on the crowd.

"And another thing," went on the puncher, who had

an Indian cast of countenance and a dangerous glint in his eye, "they've barred all us straymen, too—although I wouldn't eat with them, nohow! Old Sowbelly Johnson has spoiled more good grub than any round-up cook in the West. What you git ain't worth two-bits!"

"Oho!" laughed Bowman, slapping his leg, "so this is Sowbelly Johnson! The minute he told me to take my horse out of camp I knowed I'd seen him, somewhere. He used to cook for the Diamond A!"

He chuckled reminiscently as he poured out a cup of coffee and reached for the sugar and canned milk.

"Every morning when he'd wake 'em up he'd sing a song like this—jest as sweet!

" 'Git up and hear the little birdies sing their praise to—' And then he'd turn around and the way he'd cuss them pore cowboys was scandalous. But he shore could make good bread!"

He picked up a biscuit as he spoke and filled his plate with beans and beef.

"And every time some cowboy would come up to the fire he'd pour a big shovelful of coals right behind him and set a Dutch oven down on it.

" 'Oh, that's all right!' he'd say. 'Don't move—don't move!' "

"That's him!" whooped the strayman, and in the laugh that followed Bowman sat down and began to eat. Even Sowbelly relaxed his cynical sneer and indulged in the semblance of a smile.

"Say, where hev I seen you before?" he asked. "I

know every man that I ever cooked for and you never worked for the Diamond A."

"Yes, I did!" declared the stranger, mysteriously. "Don't you remember that little horse-wrangler that used to drag up the wood for you and help you wipe the dishes? That was me, Cusi, before I growed up. But now I'm a champion steer-roper and an A-1 bronk-rider—the best damned cowboy in the country!"

"Hear him talk!" scoffed Tex McMullen, who had been regarding him searchingly. "I'm the champion steer-roper of the *world.* I win first money last year at Pendleton and Cheyenne. What's the best time *you* ever made?"

"Sixteen seconds!" stated Bowman soberly. "And I was drunk and forgot my hogging-strings. Had to tie him with my handkerchief."

"Hear him lie!" yelped McMullen. "The best time in the world is twenty-two and three-fifths seconds, and that was made by *me.* Any time you beat that, Mister Long Rope, you can have my shirt and my *job.* But we don't need no sagebrush champs around here!"

"I wouldn't have your shirt—nor your job, either," retorted Long Rope. "Not if I had to work for this outfit. But I'll bet you a thousand dollars I can tie ten steers while you're tying one that I'd pick. I'd ketch one of these old, longhorned mountain steers and he'd run you clean out of the arena!"

"Heh! I can beat him, too!" laughed the strayman.

"These fellers ain't nothing but showmen. They can't make a hand in the hills. And say, Pardner, I remember you, now. You won first money at Túcumcari last Fourth—in roping and riding bronks!"

"Oh—*Túcumcari!*" shrilled McMullen. "So that's where you guys got your start! That's how come you're the champeens of the world! Well, every one of us boys is a genuwine champion and we've got the records to prove it. If we didn't have the goods we couldn't work with the Show. The Colonel don't take on no pikers."

"No! You bet your life!" echoed the crowd, taking courage; but Bowman only winked at the strayman.

"I remember you, Shorty," he said. "You won first money roping calves, on that little yaller horse over there."

"You bet ye!" grinned Shorty. "Joe Barfoot is the name. And that's my little Punkin hawse. I see you're still riding Brown Jug."

He nodded towards the brown that Mace had tied to a bush and Bowman swelled with pride.

"That's the best little cutting horse in New Mexico," he stated. "Ain't you, Jug?" And the brown cocked his ears.

"We-ell, boys," drawled Tex, rising up and stretching. "Let's go and leave 'em talk. Because that's where they're at their best. Why don't they come to the Rodeo next month if they're the champeen ropers of the West?"

"That's just where I'm going," announced Bowman.

"But I'll tell you what I'll do. We'll turn out ten steers and see who ties the most. Right here! For a thousand dollars—cash!"

The showmen glanced around and grinned wisely at each other and as a barrel-chested cowboy came loping in from the herd McMullen jerked his head.

"Talk to him, Mister Long Rope," he suggested. "Mortimer Steen, Chief of Cowboys in Colonel Jones's Western Shows!"

He announced his boss with such a fulsome flourish that the Chief responded with a bow; but Joe Barfoot laughed insultingly.

"That's him!" he jeered. "Chief chopping-block to the Colonel. But we call him Satchel Vest. Look at that calfskin vest he's wearing around to hang his gold medals on! And never roped a steer in his life!"

"What's the matter with *you,* Little Joe?" inquired Steen in the voice of a ballyhoo announcer. "Now you boys go out and help hold the herd while the rest come in and eat."

"All right," responded McMullen, leaping up. "But before we go, Mort, I'd like to introduce you to the Cham-peen Roper of the Wor-rld! *Mis*-ter Long Rope of Túcumcari, riding the chuck-line for his health! Hah, hah!" And he ran to catch his horse.

"That's right—laugh hearty!" Mace Bowman called after him. "But what about that bet?"

"What bet?" demanded Mortimer Steen.

"Aw, he bet me a thousand dollars, when he hasn't got the price of a meal. Jest putting up a conversation to stand off the cook for a feed. I wouldn't waste my time on no Scissors Bill like that!"

He swung up on his fine horse with a contemptuous laugh and galloped away towards the herd, and the Chief of Cowboys dismounted.

"What's this?" he demanded, walking over to Long Rope. "Can't you pay the cook for your meal?"

"Why, sure!" returned Bowman. "But you've been around some—did they collect in advance at Delmonico's?"

"Well, no!" rumbled Steen, swelling importantly. "But our orders are cash in advance! Colonel Jones sees no reason why he should feed all these straymen, or cowboys riding the line—"

"I've been around myself some," broke in Bowman, rising up, "and let me tell *you* something, Mister Satchel Vest. This is the first cow outfit that I've ever even heard of that charged for meals at the wagon."

"And that ain't the worst of it," chipped in Little Joe Barfoot. "I'm barred from the wagon because they claim I branded a maverick. But every danged maverick that they gather on the round-up they brand into the Hash-knife iron. They're eating stolen beef right now. And old Colonel Jones on the Cattle Sanitary Board, that is supposed to put a stop to sech doings! The law says all mavericks and *orejanos* shall be turned over to the Sanitary Board—"

"Say, will you shut up?" thundered Steen. "That's got nothing to do with the case. What I want to know is why this man here eats if he hasn't got the price of a meal!"

"Yes, and I want my money—right now!" barked Sowbelly. "Either that or put down yore plate."

"Well, lemme see," began Bowman, fumbling meditatively from pocket to pocket. "Now what did I do with that roll? Nope, that's just a drink-check. Ah, here we are!" And he fetched out a bill from his vest.

"Little prize money I won," he explained as the cook stared in surprise at the yellow-back. "Of course you've got the change?"

"How much is it?" asked Sowbelly, opening a drawer in his chuck-box and producing a greasy sack.

"One thousand dollars," stated Long Rope. "First prize for roping steers at Dallas."

"Let me see that bill!" demanded Steen, suddenly interested. But Long Rope drew it back.

"Lemme see the change!" he countered; and Little Joe began to laugh.

"Ee-hoo!" he whooped. "He beat the game, by grab. A thousand dollar bill to pay for a two-bit meal! Wait till I tell that to the boys over in El Toro!"

"Now here," began Steen, his eyes beginning to glint as Sowbelly whispered in his ear. "I want to examine that bill."

"And I say it's stolen!" yapped Sowbelly vindictively as he rummaged out a dusty old pistol.

"Never mind!" challenged Barfoot, suddenly rising to his feet and whipping out his six-shooter. "You Sowbelly—put up that gun. I say that there bill is O.K.

And I say it belongs to this man, until you put up the change. Does anyone here object?"

He cocked his eye up at Steen, who shook his head sullenly, and fixed Sowbelly with a venomous glance.

"No wonder," he said, "they call you the Strychnine Outfit. You're so pisen mean the coyotes wouldn't eat you. You'd rob a pore tumblebug of his little ball of dirt and put him on the wrong road home. But you don't see that bill. Understand?

"Well, come on, Pardner," he grinned, backing off. "We might as well be drifting." And, laughing, they rode off west.

CHAPTER II THE MAN FROM TÚCUMCARI

WHAT'S the matter with them fellers?" inquired Bowman as he and Barfoot topped the first roll.

"*You* ought to know," answered Little Joe. "There was a bank robbed over in Texas last week."

"I see," nodded Long Rope, looking back. "And they've got their eye on the reward."

"Yep—five hundred dollars," responded Barfoot. "But you're all right with me, understand."

"Oh, sure—sure!" nodded Long Rope absently; and drew the bill out of his pocket. "Take a look," he said, passing it over.

"Well, what's the joke?" inquired Joe as the man from Túcumcari laughed.

"It ain't signed!" chuckled Mace. "That bill is no

good. I won it in a poker game—for ten dollars."

Little Joe looked it over and passed it back doubtfully.

"You'd better put that up," he advised. "What's the idee—carrying it around?"

"Oh, just for a joke on hombres like old Sowbelly—trying to make me pay for that meal! I put my thumb over the place where the names are and flash it for a bluff."

"What's the matter—are you broke?" asked Joe.

"Nope, I had plenty of money. But when I see what a snide outfit they were, I laid myself out to beat 'em. All that talk I put up about working for the Diamond A was nothing but a bluff. Never seen old Sowbelly in my life—just heard the punchers talk about him!"

"You shore fooled him!" observed Little Joe admiringly. "I knowed you was up to something. But them Hash-knife boys are short sports and poor losers, so what say we hit the wind?"

"All right!" agreed Mace. "Straight ahead to the monument. Brown Jug wants to get a drink."

"You want to look out, around that ranch," ventured Barfoot, as they loped off across the swells. "Things ain't like they were when John Marley was there, and outside men ain't welcome."

"All I want is a drink," answered Long Rope. "Don't reckon they charge for that!"

"No, but they've got a big blacksmith, right there at the gate, and every man that comes has to fight him. You can talk all you want to and git down and say your prayers, but he won't take 'No' for an answer. He's licked everybody that's come by, up to date; and between times, just to keep his hand in, he beats up his wife and children."

"Working for Jones?" asked Bowman at last.

"He's the bouncer for Western Shows. A big, blue-faced wild Irishman with hands that reach down to his knees and hair on his breast like a dog. Kind of a cross between a sheepherder and a chimpanzee and hates cowboys like horny toads. If you don't fight he'll whip you anyway, unless you happen to outrun him."

"You don't say!" observed Long Rope, reining in. "But what do they have him around for? To keep some poor cowboy from going to the cook-house and bumming a little grub?"

"Hell, no!" laughed Barfoot. "To protect Little Eva. All the cowboys in the country come to see her."

Bowman stopped his horse short and stared.

"Who's Little Eva?" he asked.

"The prettiest little girl in all Texas!" declared Joe. "And now she's moved into New Mexico. They struck oil on the Colonel's old ranch, so he bought out the Hash-knife iron. Got to have some place to keep his horses and hands. But all the rascals do is bust other people's steers and make eyes at Little Eva. But if Martin Gilhooly sees 'em he shore makes 'em hard to ketch. The Colonel is afraid she'll git married, and that would break up the Show."

"I see," nodded Long Rope. "She's some kind of a performer."

"Performer!" hooted Joe. "She's the Colonel's daughter—the best trick and fancy rider in the Show. The cowboys come in for hundreds of miles around, just to see her jump through the loops. She's as pretty as a picture and the sweetest little thing! My Lord, if I was only about forty pounds heavier I'd tackle Gilhooly again!"

"Again!" echoed Bowman. "Did he whip you?"

"He shore did—I'll have to admit it. He could crack all your ribs at one hug. But they say Little Eva don't like him, for keeping all the cowboys away, and she's passed the word along that the first man who whips him will get a kiss from her. But he's too dam' big—I cain't cut it."

"Huh, I'll just whip him for you, if it's any accommodation. And you can have the kiss to boot. I haven't lost any pretty girls. It's good horses that ketch my eye."

"I can show you the prettiest horse in the world—and he belongs to the first man that ropes him—but you wouldn't look twice at Whistling Rufus if Eva Jones was around. She's got big, blue eyes and curly, yellow hair—used to be Little Eva in *Uncle Tom's Cabin* before she got her growth. But that's what I like—she's little, like me. I'd give my best horse for one kiss."

"Well, take me out and show me this Whistling Rufus and I'll lick the Mick with one hand. But mind you, the horse is mine."

"All right, you can have him. He's a big, blood-bay stallion with a tail that drags the ground, and his mane halfway to his knees. I know where he runs but none of us can ketch him. There ain't a fence nor a rope that will hold him."

"I'll ketch him," promised Mace, "if I ever get my eye on him. Running mustangs is just play for me. But what kind of a fight does this Irishman put up? Does he kick, or bite, or strike?"

"He grabs you!" shuddered Joe, "with them long, gorilla arms and squeezes your ribs till they crack. Then he takes you and throws you into the Bottomless Spring and all them cheap cowboys laff!"

"You watch me!" nodded Bowman. "I'll hit him so hard he'll think he's shoeing a bronk. What else does the rascal do?"

"Well, he's got a big, wiry beard—they call him Bluebeard—and when he gits you in his arms he jams that right into your eye. Then he works it around like a scrubbing-brush until you holler: 'Enough!' "

"That's one word," announced Long Rope, "that I've never said yet; so we'll ride in and give him a try. But there's one thing, Shorty, that I want you to promise. If I lick this gorilla and throw him into the spring I want you to be right there. Don't go hiding behind me if Little Eva comes out and offers to give me a kiss, because that's strictly out of my line. But when it comes to whipping blacksmiths that beat up their wives there's where Old Man Bowman's boy shines. I'll ride him with the spurs until he bawls like a calf. I'll make him bleat like a goat. And then I'll throw *him* into the Bottomless Spring. After that we'll go ketch that horse."

CHAPTER III THE WILD IRISHMAN

ON a high swell ahead, beckoning them on to the Bottomless Spring, the great monument rose gleaming white. Mace Bowman swung down and picked up a stone to add to the ever-growing pile, but Little Joe only sighed.

"That old monument used to look mighty good to me," he said, "when the Marley boys owned the ranch; but now it's pisen to see it. It jest makes me think of Eva, and old Bluebeard sitting at the gate. Colonel Jones is swelled up worse than ever since they struck oil on his Texas land, but with all his money and fine horses he's nothing but a circus-man. He treats every man that comes along like he was trying to crawl under the tent."

"I'd just like to meet that old stiff," observed Bowman, "and tell him what I think of him. It makes my blood boil every time I think of them, trying to collect that measly two-bits. And right out here, on the Staked Plains, where lots of men have died on the trail!"

"Yes, and down at the ranch it's worse," went on Joe, "with this Martin Gilhooly around. They say he came from New York, from some waterfront saloon where he threw out drunks by day's works. And he's got the meanest, insultingest way—he always calls me The Injun."

"That ain't a bad name," asserted Mace judiciously. "Lots of people around here have got a little Comanche blood, and proud of it."

"Well, that's all right—I'm proud of it, too. But Little Eva's father is a Breckenridge from Kentucky on his mother's side, and Injun blood don't go. I believe he's give orders to that blacksmith to work me over on sight."

"Never mind about him," said Long Rope confidently. "I'll grab him by the beard if he gets gay with me and snatch him bald-headed as a bat. Old Colonel Jones don't need to be so proud. The Randolphs of Virginia are just as good as he is, and all they can talk about is their Pocahontas blood that came down from the early days. But I'm sure going to fix it so one little Injun gets a kiss from the Colonel's daughter. That is, if she's a girl of her word."

"She shore is!" grinned Joe, "and I'll tell you something, Pardner—she thinks a whole lot of Little Joe. We're both little, savvy, and that goes a long ways. I'll never have no girl that's taller than I am—because the first thing she'll do if she ever wants to tease me is reach down and pat me on the head. I ain't very big, but by grab, I'm no kid. I'm a man, and an A-1 cowboy!"

"I believe you," nodded Bowman, "and it's no more than right that Little Eva should have her chance. If she wants to have a feller, and to give him a kiss, we'll throw this blacksmith out on his ear. I hate the whole outfit, ever since that greasy cook tried to shake me down for two-bits."

"But she's got a good mother," interposed Little Joe as they rode up and threw their rocks on the pile. "Merry Hart is her name and she works with the show, too. She's the Champion Rifle-shot of the World."

"We're all champions," observed Mace, looking down into the swale where the bottomless spring welled up. "But holy smoke, they've got everything changed around!"

"That's her house, up on the hill!" volunteered Joe. "And that's Eva, down in the ring!"

He pointed an eager hand at a slim girl on a white horse, cantering slowly around a tanbark ring; but Bowman did not look.

"Where's the old house?" he asked. "And the bunkhouse and corrals?"

"All gone," responded Barfoot. "The Colonel tore them down and used the stones to build that wall. Oh, the Hash-knife has gone to hell, and some people say he's even going to tear down the monument."

"The monument!" shrilled Bowman. "He'll never do that. The old-timers would rise up and kill him. Now I tell you what you do, Joe—you stay up here while I ride down and give Jug a drink. And when you hear me yell: *'Túcumcari!'* you come down and get that kiss."

He grinned and jumped Brown Jug into a lope and rode down the long slope to the spring. It welled up clear and cold from the dark depths of Mother Earth, walled in by a low curb of limestone—a famous place, well-beloved by all who knew it. But now all but the spring was changed. A new house stood on the hill, shut off by a stone wall. A long bunkhouse, painted railroad-red, flanked its base; and in place of the old ranch-house, torn down for the rocks, a cheap shack stood by the gate. It was the lurking-place of Gilhooly, the blacksmith.

As he sat his horse and took note of each change, Long Rope was aware of a movement inside the shack, which had wide cracks between the rough boards. Then a bearded countenance appeared in the open window and he saw the wild Irishman, face to face. His beard was blue-black, his bony head clipped close, and in his deep-sunk eyes there was a look of animal savagery that made Bowman's blood run cold. He was like some huge monkey in a show.

Gilhooly stared and turned away, and from the half-open shed there came the measured clank of a hammer. Then Brown Jug raised his head, sighing deep as the water trickled down from his lips, and Mace stepped off for a drink. But he drank only a sup, for he knew without telling that soon he would need all his strength. There was that about Bluebeard which made Little Joe's stories seem suddenly far short of the truth. So he drank and remounted, while Jug sipped again, and from the horse-ring he heard a low laugh. Then, boldly upright on the broad back of a white horse, Little Eva cantered gracefully into view.

In the sawdust ring the hoofbeats of the circus pony

were muffled to a distant thud; he galloped sedately with short, mincing strides; and as Eva made sure that her audience was looking she built a small loop in her rope. It grew larger and rose up, like a corona above her head, sunk low and was spun up higher; then she whipped the loop towards her and leapt through it deftly, still riding at the slow, measured lope.

"Pretty work!" yelled Mace as she glanced back for approval; and Little Eva bowed and smiled. But at that first, bold shout the watchful blacksmith came out, casting his grimy leather apron aside.

"Hey!" he bellowed. "Be on your way, young man. You've had your drink, so don't be standing there and staring at your betters."

Mace glanced at him briefly, then turned to the horse-ring where Little Eva was passing close. She was clad in silk tights, her yellow curls dancing as she rode, and on her face there was a sweet, wistful smile. She held up her hand after the fashion of trick riders, then vaulted to the ground, swung up on the horse and dropped down on the other side. She mounted up, beaming, raised her hand again, and with a plunge and a struggle clambered under her horse's neck and up on the other side. Mace clapped his hands as she made her bow; and she galloped off, looking back.

Then for the first time the cowboy was aware of a presence that stood beside him. It was the bouncer, grinning evilly.

"What's your business here, young feller?" he

asked. “This is private property, the estate of Colonel Jones, and no trespassers are allowed.”

“Were you speaking to me?” inquired Bowman, looking around; and Gilhooly caught a big breath.

“I shure was!” he roared, “and I’ll not say it again. You’re no b’iler-maker and you heard me the first time. Be arf, before I put ye arf! I can whip any man that wears spurs.”

“You don’t say!” responded Mace. “Have you whipped all these jaspers around here?”

He pointed to a circle of dissipated-looking show-hands who had appeared like magic from their hiding-places, and the blacksmith eyed them contemptuously.

“I’ve learned them their place!” he barked, “and to mind their own business and not stand staring while Eva, the little dahrling, does her tricks.”

He looked over as he spoke to the corner of the horse-ring, and Little Eva made a face at him.

“Heh!” laughed Bowman, “when they rope and ride like she does a cowboy can’t help but watch. That’s real riding, ain’t it, boys?”

The blacksmith turned his sledge-hammer head and glared at the crestfallen show-hands, who promptly slunk away. Then he raised his big fist and struck it into his open hand while he let out a bawl like a bull.

“Hey!” he demanded. “Do you know who I am? I’m Martin Gilhooly, the boss bouncer of Western Shows! And when I say ‘Go’ you want to *Go!* When I saw your shoulders I thought maybe you might be a fighter, but one look in your face and I knew I was mistaken. You're afraid to step down and fight me—but only a friendly bout, of course!"

"When I fight a friendly bout," answered Long Rope sarcastically, "I'll fight it with a friend. A cowboy don't get down and roll in the dirt like a dog with every Irish Mick he comes across. But I'll bet you a thousand dollars I can whip you, fist and skull, all tripping and wrastling barred!"

"You ain't got no thousand dollars—nor ten dollars, ayther. But you'll get down, young feller, and fight me, or I'll throw you into the spring!"

"You lay a hand on me," warned Mace, "and I'll crack your States Prison head with this gun-barrel. I ain't afraid of no lowbrowed Hibernian, and after seeing you I believe every word of that story about Saint Patrick. It seems a shipload of monkeys was wrecked on the coast of Old Ireland, and the British sent out a regiment of soldiers to shoot them before they spread. But at the end of the first day they'd killed more Micks than monks. Then Saint Patrick said: 'Let every true Irishman wear a four-leafed clover so the soldiers can tell you apart.' And ever since that time, on Saint Patrick's day, the Irish wear a clover in their hats."

He threw back his head and laughed, and Little Eva laughed with him; but the roustabouts turned and fled, lest they draw down the anger of Bluebeard.

"Niver mind your dhirty cracks about the Irish!" he bellowed. "I can lick you with wan hand behind me back!"

"You couldn't lick a postage stamp," jeered Bowman, "let alone a man like me. I'm a gentleman, savvy? I don't fight for fun. But I'll bet a thousand dollars, as I said before, that I can make you holler: 'Enough!' "

"You ain't got no thousand dollars—nor ten! So put up or shut up, you rapscallion!"

"All right," nodded Long Rope, reaching into his vest pocket and fetching out his thousand dollar bill. "Just cover that, Squirley, or I'll be on my way." And he flashed the yellow-back in the sun.

There was a moment of awed silence as a roustabout edged closer and read the figures on the bill.

"That's right," he said. "It's a grand."

"I won that over at Dallas," observed Mace, confidentially. "First money in the steer-roping contest."

He backed his horse around, showing the plate on his cantle, and headed him out the gate.

"Wa-ait a minute!" challenged Gilhooly, dashing out in front of him. "You'll fight me, after that!"

"Sure I'll fight you!" assented Long Rope, "but not for the pleasure of having you bite my ear. I've heard about you, Bluebeard, and your dirty, barroom tricks; but I'll match you for ten dollars, no holt barred."

"I haven't got ten dollars!" wailed the bouncer, almost in tears. "But just let me lay me hands on ye!"

"All right," agreed Mace. "I'll bet you ten dollars against your anvil, just to show the little lady a good fight."

He bowed to Eva, who nodded encouragingly, and the blacksmith rolled up his sleeves.

"Get down," he said tremulously, "and lave me at ye. We'll see who hollers: 'Enough!' "

"Just a friendly bout!" warned Long Rope as he dismounted and took off his gun-belt. "Here, Mister, hold this ten dollars. If I win, the old anvil is mine."

"That's agreed," nodded Gilhooly, grinning expectantly. "I can whip anny man that wears spurs."

Bowman took off his hat and hung it on his saddle-horn, then jumped up, jingling his rowels.

"Come on!" he whooped. "I'll ride you like a goat. I'm from Túcumcari! Whoopeelah!"

CHAPTER IV HAMMER AND TONGS

GILHOOLY came charging, his long, hairy arms reaching out to drag Bowman down. He was a rough-and-tumble, waterfront battler, trained to grapple and gouge and slug; but Long Rope had fought bronks and outlaw bulls and his instinct was to dodge and evade. He jumped sidewise like a cat, turned and swirled and ducked again until Gilhooly howled with rage. Then he stood up and hit him with all his strength and the bouncer sat down in the dirt. But he rose up, shaking his head, and plunged in again, and once more the cowboy danced away.

A cloud of dust eddied about as they raced in and out, now standing face to face to exchange bruising blows, now clutching and breaking away. But always it was the blacksmith who rushed and pursued and the cowboy who dodged or slugged. When he struck he put his whole body behind it, and Gilhooly began to labor and grunt. He was a bulldog for strength and ferocity, but the greyhound was wearing him down. Then a monkey-like paw groped out and clutched, and Long Rope fought to escape.

Two arms like iron bands closed in on his ribs and locked him in a deadly embrace. They stumbled and went down, rolling and bumping their heads, lost from sight in the dust of battle. But in or out, the strong arms hugged him closer and the rough beard scrubbed against his face. Bowman reached up and grabbed it, pushing it back with all his strength while he took to the blacksmith with his spurs.

A loud yell went up as the sharp steel rowels hooked the back of the bouncer's legs. He struggled to get free, but Long Rope raked him till he bucked and squealed like a bronk. Then, as Gilhooly squirmed frantically, he grabbed him from behind and clamped down on him with his horse-breaking knees. Their vise-like grip, which had tamed many an outlaw, crushed the blacksmith's ribs till they cracked; but all the time as if riding in a contest Mace kept his spurs in play.

Gilhooly rose up, fighting desperately to escape, to shake off this incubus, this Old Man of the Sea, who gripped him in the iron clamp of his knees; but with loud, triumphant shouts Bowman rode him and roweled him until they crashed against the wall of the shop. They tumbled in, wall and all, and as hammers and tongs came raining down Mace lost his grip and backed out. But a long, hairy arm snatched him down into the cinders and, striking blindly, they grappled again.

Mace felt the cruel arms choking out his very life, he felt a hot breath against his cheek; then into his left eye like a thousand red-hot needles he felt the thrust of the bristling beard. Fighting furiously to get away from it he pushed with both hands to shove the rough jowls away; but Gilhooly had him in his old, familiar grip and there was nothing left but the spurs. Long Rope grappled and raked him with both rowels and the blacksmith let go with a yelp.

They rose up in the wreckage and closed like angry dogs, and at the first tumbling charge the back wall went down, pinning them in under the sagging roof. But Bowman was on top now and with a lightning turn he clamped down on Gilhooly from behind.

"Now I've got you!" he whooped, sinking his spurs into both legs; and in the roughriding that followed, the last wall bulged out and the blacksmith hollered:

"Enough!"

Then the roof fell on the top of them, making the ruin complete, and Long Rope bulled his way out.

"Did you hear that?" he inquired of the world at large. "Gilhooly says: 'Enough!' I'm from Túcumcari! Whoopeelah!"

He laughed raucously as he turned and, laying hold

of the weighty anvil, he lifted it block and all and staggered towards the spring.

"There goes old Bluebeard!" he announced as he heaved it into the depths; and from the horse-ring there came a patter of applause. Little Eva was standing tiptoe on the back of her white horse, blowing kisses and beckoning him to come.

A sudden silence fell as she leapt down and started towards him and Mace stared wildly about.

"Oh, Joe!" he shouted. "Hurry up! *Túcumcari!*"

But Little Joe was nowhere to be seen. There was just a gang of show-hands, striving weakly to free the blacksmith; and Little Eva, smiling expectantly.

"That's all right, Lady," he began as she glanced up at him coquettishly, "I heard there was a kind of a reward for the man that whipped this Mick. But with this eye he gave me, if it's all the same to you—"

"Nay, no, Sir Knight!" she chided, mischievously. "I never go back on my word. Kneel down, so I can reach you—"

"Just a minute!" protested Long Rope, standing tall. "As I was about to say, it was a pleasure to lick him and I couldn't accept no reward. But if you must keep your word, here's my little friend—"

He looked around, just as Barfoot jumped down off his horse.

"Come up here!" ordered Mace, nabbing Joe by the collar. "Come up and take the reward!"

He held him, in case he weakened, and Little Eva

kissed him gravely. Then as Bowman let him go she twined her arms about his neck and gave him an ecstatic kiss.

"I keep my word!" she laughed. "And it's a pleasure to do it. But look out—here comes Dad!"

Down the road from the big house, running faster at every jump, a tall, slim man came galloping upon them, his long hair flying out behind. His flowing white mustache and goatee, his high boots and flashing black eyes, made him look like Buffalo Bill—and he cursed like Buffalo Bill. But to Bowman he was only a cheap show-man and he waited, grinning expectantly.

"What's this?" yelled the Colonel, looking wildly into the spring-hole. "Did you throw Gilhooly in?"

"Oh, no," answered Mace. "He's under the roof."

"But I heard you say: 'There goes old Bluebeard!' And I saw you throw him into the spring!"

"Oh, Dad, that was the *anvil!*" cried Eva, beginning to laugh. "He just said that for a *joke!*"

"What—what? Did he throw in my anvil! And is this another joke—making a wreck of my blacksmith shop?"

"You ought to see your blacksmith," grinned Long Rope. "The big yap thought he could whip me."

"Pull me out!" howled Gilhooly from under the wreckage. "He's bruk ivery bone in me body, and tore me to pieces with his spurs."

He struggled out from beneath the toppling roof and as Little Eva beheld him she burst into a merry laugh.

"You go back to your mother!" ordered the Colonel severely. And then he turned on Mace.

"Who are you, sir?" he demanded. "And what the devil do you mean, destroying all my property?"

"Yes, and look at me shop!" quavered the blacksmith as he pawed the cinders out of his eyes. "And me anvil—trun down the spring!"

"That's all right," defended Bowman, striding over to a roustabout and swiftly reclaiming his ten dollars. "I bet this ten against your anvil, and I reckon you'll admit you're whipped!"

"That has nothing to do with it!" stormed Colonel Jones. "The anvil was not his—it was mine! Now what is your name, sir, and who's going to pay me for all this damage to my property?"

"I'm Mace Bowman, from Túcumcari, the Champion Steer Roper of the World!"

"Oh, indeed?" sneered the Colonel. "What about Tex McMullen? I suppose you're seeking a job?"

"What—with you?" shrilled Mace. "Don't you never think it. A man that's so cheap he charges for meals is too damned cheap for me. I just came in here to show up your blacksmith and tell you what I thought of your spread."

"Well, you get out of here!" commanded Jones. "Get off of my property. I've a good mind to have you arrested."

"Go ahead and arrest, if you think you can cut it. But you'll have to ketch me first. You and your Main Street cowboys and your tough saloon bouncer!

Here's a bunch of whiskers I jerked out of his beard. You might use 'em to stuff a pillow."

He threw down an imaginary handful of hair and reined his horse away, laughing.

He was galloping off when, on the back of her white horse, he saw Eva, waving her hand ecstatically.

"Good-by!" he hollered, waving back at her. But Little Joe was waving, too.

CHAPTER V THE BEEFSTEAK

LONG ROPE was under a spell as he loped off down the road and turned west towards El Toro and the Pecos. The sun shone with dazzling splendor, there was a rainbow in the sky; and before him like a bird of good omen a scissor-tailed flycatcher soared. Her ashy body was dashed with crimson, her head was scarlet-crowned; and her long, long tail-feathers trailed out behind like a gorgeous wedding train.

The kiss that Eva had given him had gone to his head like wine. He was drunk with ecstasy and the wild joy of battle, and his injuries were all forgotten. But of course she was Little Joe's girl.

"By grab, Pardner!" exclaimed Joe, riding up beside him, "you sure put that blacksmith on the bum. But say—Little Eva! Ain't she the prettiest girl you ever saw? And she came right up and kissed me, like I was a gentleman and a scholar. I ain't no Injun to her."

"Well, she kissed me, too," said Long Rope. "But

she had to climb my neck to do it. Why, hell, Joe—she's nothing but a child. She hasn't got her growth yet."

"Yes, she has!" asserted Little Joe vehemently. "I reckon I ought to know—she ain't growed an inch in two years. I seen her the first time she came into this country—she was mounted on that little white horse—and she ain't a bit bigger today."

"No, but listen! She was riding a *big* horse today, and that's what made her look small. I'll bet she outgrows you, yet."

"Aw, shut up," scoffed Joe, "and lemme look at that eye. Say, Big Boy, it's almost closed!"

"That's where that wild Irishman bored a hole with his chin. He's the hardest man to handle that I ever tackled—I'm bruised from my somber to my heels."

"But you shore tore the hide off of him with them spurs," praised Barfoot. "I rode down where I could watch. When he crawled out from under that blacksmith shop he looked like two-bits' worth of dog meat."

"Well, I feel like I'd been drug through a barbed-wire fence, myself, and kicked in the ribs to boot. But this eye is the only place that hurts bad."

"Leave it to me!" nodded Joe. "I'll fix you up. What you need for that eye is a good, big beefsteak, and I'm the man to git it. You done me a favor that I won't soon forget, so lay down—and watch my dust."

He waved his hand towards a spreading mesquite tree and turned out into the brush where a bunch of cattle stood, head up. They scampered off before him but as Mace stretched out he heard the loud whang of a six-shooter. A few minutes later Little Joe came spurring back and handed him a big, bloody steak.

"Put that over your eye and take a rest," he said, "while I go back and butcher that beef. I'm out of meat, anyhow, so we'll jest wrap it up and take it along to the ranch."

"All right," agreed Bowman, pressing the steak to his throbbing eye; but just as the pain eased and he was dozing off he heard the distant drumming of hoofs. There was haste in their rapid tattoo, and a suggestion of danger, and he rose up to look around. Out in the brush Little Joe had wrapped the beef in his slicker and was hoisting it up on his horse, but the hammer of flying hoofs had turned into a thunder that spoke of headlong pursuit. Mace straightened up and with lightning rapidity snatched the thousand dollar bill from his pocket. Then, prying open a hidden slit in the lining of his bootleg, he tucked it deftly inside.

The next moment Colonel Jones on a magnificent white stallion came galloping around the bend, and behind him followed Satchel Vest and Tex.

"Um-huh!" grunted Long Rope, "they're out for that reward."

Then he stretched out and waited, grimly.

They came in neck and neck, each racing to be the first, but as Mace stood up and raised his hands negligently, Tex McMullen spied Little Joe. With a twist of the wrist he reined his horse aside and they all turned to watch for a fight. He drew his pistol as he charged and Joe Barfoot, looking back, had his right hand on his gun; but as the cowboy dashed up Joe let the beef fall and stood crestfallen, hands in the air.

"They've killed a yearling!" shouted back Tex after he had snatched away Barfoot's six-shooter; and, grabbing at the slicker, he dumped the meat into the dirt.

"Yee-hoo!" he whooped. "Look at that brand! It's a Hash-knife! The rascals were stealing beef!"

"Bring him over here!" ordered the Colonel, smiling triumphantly; and Little Joe came, head down.

"That's a slick-ear," he said as he halted before Jones and cast an anxious glance to Mace. "Some feller has sleepered it—I thought it was a maverick. Never seen the brand till afterwards. But this man here had nothing to do with it—I just killed it to get a steak for his eye!"

"Ah, hah, hah!" yelled McMullen, "that's pretty good, hey? Then what the devil was you wrapping it up for, and tying it on your saddle?"

"Well, I didn't want to waste it!" defended Little Joe weakly; and the Colonel and his Chief joined the laugh.

"You'll have to think up a better lie than that," observed Jones, letting down his rope. "Tie him up, boys, before he escapes."

"Well, that's the truth!" stated Bowman. "He never went to steal. But my eye hurt so bad I asked him for a beefsteak. Here it is—you can see for yourselves."

He produced the thick steak and Colonel Jones eyed

him arrogantly, while his henchmen awaited his will.

"Tie him up, too," he said. "He's a dangerous criminal. But wait just a minute—we'll search him for evidence. I'm satisfied he's one of those bank robbers."

"Who—me?" protested Long Rope. "Why would I rob a bank?"

"To git the money!" yelped McMullen, in great good humor. "I claim half of that reward, Mort!"

"You're both in my employ," barked the Colonel, "and the reward for this capture goes to me."

McMullen reared back and faced him, a retort on his lips; then he mumbled to himself and searched Bowman's pockets, but without any notable results.

"Where's that thousand dollar bill you flashed on the cook?" he asked as he came to Mace's boots.

"Why, right there in my jumper pocket," responded Long Rope, innocently; and both of them grabbed at once.

"It ain't there," rumbled Satchel Vest, at last. "Let's strip him and frisk him good."

"I had it back at the ranch!" declared Bowman, "because I flashed it on that blacksmith. What's the matter? It's perfectly good."

"I'll bet he lost it in that fight!" exclaimed Tex, jumping up. "Let's go back and search the shop!"

"Now here!" warned Mace. "That's my bill, understand! I won it at Dallas—first money in steer-roping—and by grab I want it back!"

"You won't need any money where *you're* going," sneered Tex. "You'll be making States Prison bridles, with all expenses paid. Well, how about it, Colonel? Shall I go back and look for it, or help take these prisoners to town?"

"Go and search for it," ordered Jones. "But mind you, Mr. McMullen, I want that bill for *evidence!*"

"All right," shrugged McMullen, mounting with effortless ease, "but I don't reckon we really need it. Just take along this beefsteak he was going to put on his *eye,* and the jury will do the rest. I knowed he was a cow-thief the minute I seen that *long rope!*"

He grinned impishly at Bowman, who glowered back at him hatefully, and galloped off up the trail.

"See you later, Túcumcari!" he yupped.

CHAPTER VI THE PRINCE OF BARKEEPS

THERE was no rainbow in the sky, no glory in the West, as Long Rope, his hands tied, rode the Dry Trail to the Pecos and landed in the El Toro jail. In a gay spirit of adventure he had set forth at dawn and in a quixotic mood had undertaken the task of beating the Hash-knives out of two-bits. Then to please Little Joe, his pardner in crime, he had taken on Gilhooly, the fighting blacksmith of Bottomless Spring, and won him a lover's kiss.

How bright was the sun, how joyous the world, as they galloped off down the trail! But who would have thought that, to get a steak for his eye, Little Joe would have beefed a Hash-knife calf? And then, without a word, dressed the carcass and wrapped it up and hoisted it on his horse! It would take quite a talk to a jury of cowmen to make them understand this play, and bring in a verdict of Not Guilty. And if the verdict went the other way they were elected to go to the Pen.

But Little Joe's heart was right, even though his judgment erred, and as they thundered across the bridge and rode up to the courthouse, Long Rope glanced at his pardner and smiled. Joe was a cow-thief, of course—but all the time he had believed that Long Rope was a bank robber. He probably believed it yet. What a melancholy thought that, for their misguided chivalry, they might both be sent to prison! They were examined before a magistrate on a charge of grand larceny and turned over to the custody of the sheriff, who promptly locked them up.

They stood alone inside the jail, looking out through the iron bars, and a silence fell upon them. Strange odors were about them, and strange noises of men sleeping; but everything that day had been strange.

"It'll come out all right," spoke up Little Joe at last. "I've got lots of friends in town."

"That so?" returned Mace. "Any lawyers?"

"Nope. All barkeepers," answered Joe; and Long Rope grunted as he stretched out wearily on the floor.

But in the morning as they waited for the belated breakfast, there being but two meals a day, the prince of all barkeepers came in. He was a tall, impressive man with a mustache dyed dead-black and an air of world-weary sophistication; but as he entered behind the jailer he put one thumb behind his ear and wagged his hand like the ear of a cow. It was a secret sign to Little Joe, and instantly his dark face lit up.

"Hello, Cramer," he said, "I knew you'd come. What's the chances of getting out of this hole?"

"Very good indeed, Brother Barfoot," responded the barkeep, in the bosom of whose white shirt there glowed a diamond so large that it lit up the gloom like a star. "I have already seen the sheriff. As a loyal member of the North American Improvement and Gulf Stream Diversion Company I feel confident you would do no wrong; but as a mere matter of form you will be asked to remain in jail until Colonel Jones and his henchmen leave town. Have a smoke," and he passed in a cigar.

"On the book, Brother Barfoot," he went on, "you are charged with grand larceny of a yearling calf, but of course there is some mistake. The NAI can always be depended upon to relieve any brother in distress, but if it is violating no confidence I should be very glad to know what line your defense will take."

"Well," said Joe, "I killed the calf, all right. But some crazy cow-thief had branded it, intending to ear-mark it later on. Some Hash-knife puncher is my guess. He'd branded it into the Hash-knife and left the ears slick, so I took it for a maverick.

"Well, after I'd killed it," explained Little Joe, "I didn't want to waste the meat. But just as I was tying the beef up in my slicker the Colonel and his cowboys came."

"Ah, yes," murmured the bartender, "so that's the way it was! Well, a jury of fellow members would doubtless see the justice of your plea. But another reason, not quite so utilitarian, would have a better effect on the masses."

"I'll tell you why he killed that beef," spoke up Mace, who had been standing by unnoticed. "I'd just got a black eye in a fight and he wanted to get me a beefsteak."

The gentlemanly barkeeper regarded him coldly, then turned inquiringly to Joe.

"This is a friend of mine," spoke up Barfoot. "Mace Bowman, of Túcumcari, the Champion Steer Roper of the World."

"Have a cigar, Mr. Bowman," responded Cramer, with a nod; but as Joe beckoned him closer and whispered into his ear the barkeep's eyes lit up.

"Well, well!" he exclaimed, thrusting his hand through the bars and warmly clasping Mace's. "Brother Barfoot informs me that you whipped Martin Gilhooly and threw him down a well. It's an honor to make your acquaintance—I hope the well was good and deep."

"No—no. His anvil!" prompted Joe. But Cramer was lost in laughter.

"This calls for the drinks!" he proclaimed at last, "and a special meeting—tonight. Mr. Bowman, as president and founder of the North American

Improvement Company, I welcome you into our midst and assure you that your wishes are my law. Anything that I can do, don't hesitate to name it. So you whipped him and threw him down the well!"

He shook hands again and Joe drew him closer.

"He tells me further," beamed Cramer, "that you beat the Hash-knife wagon out of a meal; and that you told them, one and all, what red-blooded Americans think of such an outrageous charge. We are having a little meeting of the NAI tonight in the back room of the Long Horn Saloon and I hope you will attend, Mr. Bowman, as the guest of honor of the evening."

"Fine and dandy," agreed Mace. "I'd be only too glad to—except for getting out of jail."

"Oh, that can be very easily arranged, I am sure. Now that you explain the human motive behind the killing of this calf it becomes, instead of grand larceny, a very praiseworthy act. I have some slight influence with our sheriff, Mordecai Byrnes—on account of a bar-bill, and so forth—and I think when he understands the circumstances you will undoubtedly be released."

He rattled the gate for the jailer and a few minutes later he returned with Mordecai Byrnes. There was a pained and jaundiced look on the thin, hatchet-like face of this minion of the law and he eyed the battered prisoner evilly as Cramer put up his talk.

"That's all very well, Mr. Cramer," he rasped, "but this man is being held under suspicion of being a bank robber. Colonel Jones requested especially that we keep him locked up until a thousand dollars that he stole is found."

"But Mordecai," reasoned the barkeep, "this gentleman is a friend of Little Joe. And *his* father was one of our oldest residents—a man with a host of friends. Are you going to take the word of this flapdoodle showman against that of Joe Barfoot—and me? I tell you, Mordecai Byrnes, this man is innocent. And furthermore, I want him released."

"We-ell," qualified the sheriff, "I'll release him into your custody. That is, if you'll go his bond."

"Good enough," agreed Cramer. "That's all I ask. Bring on your papers and I'll sign them, with pleasure. The NAI, Mr. Byrnes, will be glad to know that you consider *them*—once in a while."

"Oh, I think a whole lot of them," declared Mordecai, hastily. "But the law is the law, Mr. Cramer."

"There is something above the law," declared the barkeeper. "And that is justice, Mr. Byrnes. And there is something above all sheriffs and public officials, and that is the will of the people. As expressed through the medium of the ballot. Now if you want to stand in with these magnates like Colonel Jones, and keep all the little men in jail—"

"Hell—no!" cried Mordecai. And, throwing open the gate, he ushered Mace out like a king.

CHAPTER VII
THE MAN WHO LICKED GILHOOLY

AFTER a long sleep all day, and the services of a physician to reduce his swollen eye, Mace Bowman went down to the Long Horn Saloon with an entirely different opinion of barkeepers. In his past experience they had been the cowboy's friend as long as his money lasted, but James G. Cramer had fed him and clothed him and got him out of prison. And now, though he could hardly believe it, he was to be the guest of honor of the North American Improvement Company.

Though its purpose was still a trifle hazy, Mace could readily see that the NAI was a power in El Toro County. At the mere mention of their name and the influence they exerted, the saturnine sheriff had flung open the prison gates and let him out without bond. Many men on the street had stopped and shaken hands, many doors had been opened, many good wishes expressed—and yet he was held for a cow-thief. When the Grand Jury met he would have to go before them, and he was sure to be bound over for trial; but despite his battered countenance and the criminal charge against him, he was welcomed on every hand. He was the man who whipped Gilhooly.

Behind the resplendent bar of the Long Horn Saloon, Cramer was mixing and pouring drinks with the skill of a trained magician. He shook eggnogs and made gin-fizzes, jolted drinks out of black bottles or opened up the finest liqueurs, and all with the languid air of one who has gone far and seen much. He was the social mentor of the great cowtown of El Toro and he took Long Rope under his wing.

As he sidled into the barroom where above the great mirror an enormous pair of horns were hung, Cramer beckoned him up and shook hands. Then, turning to two gentlemen who were leaning on their elbows, he introduced them in turn.

"Mr. Bowman," he began, "as Champion Steer Roper of the World I want you to meet two of our most distinguished citizens who are also in the champion class. This is Red Tutlow, the oil magnate—the Champion Booze Fighter of New Mexico. In his time Mr. Tutlow has attained the record of sixty full glasses a day—straigh't whisky, and chasers barred, thus beating the record of Booze Buyer of Mexicali, who drinks a quart of neat whisky every night."

The Champion Booze Fighter was a small man with a husky voice and an odd, metallic gleam in his eye; but his face was illumined with an irrepressible smile and he shook hands with a merry quip.

"And now," went on Cramer, "let me introduce our other champion—Phat Noland, the Champion Roughriding Barber of Arizona, whose shop is just down the street. On the race track at Tucson Mr. Noland shaved a drunk cowboy, riding backward on a bucking bronco, and only cut his throat twice."

Phat Noland was small and dapper, with a Cupid's-bow mouth and a mischievous droop to one eye; and he winked as Mace laughed at the joke.

"I had to leave Tucson—for my health," he explained. "This cowboy had lots of friends."

With these two boon companions the time passed very pleasantly until, as the graveyard shift came on, Mr. Cramer removed his white apron. This was the signal for the chosen few of the NAI to drift back to a quiet card room, where the rest of the NAI were gathered. Little Joe and Mace were escorted in last and, as they entered, the entire membership rose up and placed their thumbs behind their ears. Then they wagged their hands like a butterfly's wings and sat down with friendly smiles. It was the sign with which Cramer had announced his friendship when he found Mace and Joe in jail.

"Gentlemen," began Cramer, grinning broadly as he took Bowman by the arm, "I take pleasure in presenting to you as our guest of honor tonight, the man who licked Gilhooly!"

A raucous cheer gave Long Rope his welcome into this band of chosen spirits and they wagged their ears again in a sort of Chautauqua salute.

"Yes, he tamed the wild Irishman, and tied him to his anvil and sunk him in the Bottomless Spring. Little Eva, the Colonel's daughter, was so delighted at the deed that she gave both him and Joe a hearty kiss. But let not that chaste salute be the sole reward for this man who has struck at Irish tyranny. I am going to ask

Brother Barfoot to propose the name of Mace Bowman for full membership in the NAI, and let there be not one dissenting vote."

Then as the motion was passed with prolonged applause Cramer turned abruptly on the neophyte. "Have you got any money?" he asked.

"Why—yes!" answered Long Rope, in surprise.

"That's all," nodded the barkeep, "the NAI goes no further. We care nothing how you acquired your roll as long as you can buy the drinks."

He pressed a button as he spoke and two white-jacketed bartenders appeared. Then as the round of drinks was paid for and the members were seated, Cramer rose and cleared his throat.

"Brother Bowman," he began, "you are now a member in good standing of the North American Improvement and Gulf Stream Diversion Company, whose purpose it is, by the diversion of ocean currents, to improve these United States. The Gulf Stream, as you know, flows up the East Coast of North America until it is met by the cold Arctic Current, which deflects it to the coast of Ireland.

"But for this deflection, New England and Nova Scotia would be a tropical paradise; and the Emerald Isle, now so fertile and green, would become a frozen wilderness. It is the purpose of this Company to throw a dam across the Strait of Belle Isle, which separates Newfoundland from the mainland. This would effectively turn aside the cold waters of the Arctic and at the same time cut off at its source the supply of Irish policemen, the greatest menace to our peace and happiness.

"Eminent engineers have been consulted and have pronounced our plans feasible. The Strait of Belle Isle is only fifteen miles across, with a mean depth of five thousand feet. Every dollar that is spent to turn aside this frozen stream is a blow struck for liberty and freedom, but until the time that our great project is accomplished we must strive to better conditions nearer home. By whipping the Wild Irishman of Bottomless Spring you have proven your right to join our Company, and to buy the drinks for the crowd."

He pressed the button again and after the refreshments had been served he rapped on a table for order.

"Our regular business meeting will now begin," he said, "and any members who wish may propose further ways of improving North America."

At this a huge, swart cowman who had drunk his whisky in silence rose up and glared about.

"Brother Hockaday," announced Cramer suavely, "pioneer cattleman of the Guadalupe Mountains."

"Mr. President," he began, "it's all right to buy the drinks and talk about that thar Gulf Stream; but they's one man, and he ain't no Irishman, that has got to be put down. I mean this Colonel Jones that bought out John Marley and tuk over the old Hash-knife iron. Thar's a thorough-paced tinhorn if ever I seen one, and them professional ropers and riders of his done broke up our Rodeo last spring.

"Hyer we go to big expense and build a fine park fur

the contest, and then them show-hands of his take all the first prizes and make our boys look like fools. They're nothing but circus hands but they've got the hawses—best rope-hawses in the country and trained fur nothing else. I think this hyer Colonel—and he's no more a Colonel than I am—and all them smart-aleck hands, ought to be barred from the contests this year and let our regular cowboys win."

He sat down, grumbling loudly in his throat like an outraged mountain bull; and Neil Monroe, the merchant, rose up. He was rotund and smiling and, as the largest contributor, was president of the El Toro Rodeo Committee.

"I agree with Ben Hockaday," he said, "that these Hash-knife men ought to be put down. It is the purpose of this Rodeo or Round-up to attract outside people to our town, so that old friends can meet and all have a good time and at the same time build up business. But last year all the prize money was won by these outsiders, who never spent a dollar if they could help it, and the merchants who subscribed got nothing. Our old customers were disappointed at the show we put on and many went home in disgust.

"But at the same time, fellow members, we can't bar these men just because they have the Hash-knife brand. We've got to figure out some other way of beating them, or cutting down on their winnings. Now for instance, in trick riding and roping, our boys haven't got a chance; so why not cut the prizes in these contests to almost nothing and put the money into steer-tying and bronk-riding? Then change the name to Pioneer Day and cut out these fancy bucking-chutes. Make 'em rope and wrastle their bronks and saddle 'em in the open the way us old-timers used to do."

"Now say, fellers," spoke up Phat Noland, "I've got an idea. Any way you can fix it, with these rope-horses they've got, them Hash-knives are going to win. They're the picked hands in the whole country and practice roping all the time, but git some big wild steers from up in the mountains and them fellers will be afraid. They won't even enter, for fear of getting hurt or having their fine cutting-horses gored. But Ben's boys, and all our cowboys, know how to handle these steers. That's the way to keep our money at home!"

"He's right!" shouted Hockaday, "and I'll get the steers myself whenever the Committee says the word. But it's a dam' shame our cowboys have got to lose in the bronk-riding to these yaps in the calfskin vests. We've got the roughriders—let's ketch a bunch of wild horses that nobody but a mustanger can touch. Some regular old bad-ones that have been fighting off the panthers until they'll kick, bite and strike all at once. When these fancy dude cowboys git into the pen with them you won't be able to see fur the dust. The blood and ha'r will fly, and I only hope some of them show-offs git killed!"

He sat down to great applause and Red Tutlow jumped up, to add a skyrocket to the joke.

"Let's ketch Whistling Rufus!" he proposed, "and saw him off on Tex McMullen. I can do that part when I pass the hat for the drawings. Just slip him the right number and he'll have to ride the man-eater or be barred from all the contests. If he rides, Rufe will kill him as sure as Gawd made little apples—and if he don't, our local boys win!"

"Yeh! Fine!" scoffed Ben Hockaday. "But who's going to ketch Rufus? I've got a standing reward of one thousand dollars fur any man that will bring him in. The finest get in the country are them mustang colts of his—he's a Steeldust stud, and I know it. But Little Joe Barfoot tried to trap him all last summer and never got him inside the wings."

"I could of done it," protested Joe, "only them cowboys of yours was all trying to snare him themselves. Jest when I had him coming some peeler would break the line and the whole dam' band would get out."

"Well, I'll tell you what I'll do," offered Hockaday. "You go over to Wild Hawse Mesa and git the band located, and when my round-up is done I'll take the whole outfit and we'll go over and try it again. I'll put up the hawses and the men and the grub, and this time they won't be no reward. All I ask for my pay is Whistling Rufus—you boys can have all the rest."

"Huh! There's no use talking to me!" complained Joe. "I'm supposed to be in jail, right now, for stealing that maverick calf."

"Well, boys will be boys," sighed Hockaday, "but you done stole him from Colonel Jones. I'm the last man in the country to stand fur rustling; but at the same time, Joe, if you'll go out after Rufus I'll go your bond and help you come clear."

"You hired a hand," agreed Barfoot. "But what about my pardner? He's a champion steer-roper and an A-1 mustanger and I want him along, to help."

"I don't know *him,*" stated Hockaday, "and I won't go his bond. But I know you, Joe, and I knowed your daddy before you. I know you won't skip out."

"Neither will he!" defended Joe. "And I done promised him, Uncle Ben, that I'd show him Whistling Rufus. He whipped that blacksmith for me, and all he asked was I'd take him to Wild Horse Mesa."

"Well, as I understand it," began Neil Monroe, "Mr. Bowman is being held on two charges. I'm always glad to help, in a case like this—and especially against these Hash-knife men—but I'd like a few more details about that thousand dollar bill."

"That's easy," laughed Mace. "I win it for ten dollars, from a cowboy that had been drifted out up north. It's an unsigned bill that somebody stole and passed on like a hot potato. Because if anybody ever caught you with that bill in your possession they'd put you in the stray-pen for life."

"Hey, heh!" chuckled the fat storekeeper, who had been a cowboy himself, "that's frank enough, I'm sure. But if it's a fair question, Mr. Bowman, I'd like to ask what happened to that bill."

"We-ell," began Mace, reaching down into his boot,

"among friends I reckon it's all right. It's supposed to be lost, but as a matter of fact I've got it right here in my boot-lining."

"Don't you show it!" ordered Monroe as the crowd began to whoop. "I don't want to know anything about it. But if you're as honest as all that, Brother Bowman, I'll arrange to go on your bond."

"Good enough!" pronounced Cramer, rising up and pressing the button. "The drinks are on the house. It is the sense of this meeting that no bill has been stolen and the NAI knows nothing about it. And now let us drink to the downfall of the Irish and the confusion of Colonel Jones. One for all and all for one, until the Hash-knives are run out of town."

CHAPTER VIII WHISTLING RUFUS

IT was a great day for Long Rope when, freed from jail, he prepared to start on the horse-hunt. His heels hardly touched as, with Little Joe, he bought supplies and provisions at Monroe & Company's store and stuffed them into the kyacks. But just as they were lashing the packs on, Colonel Jones and Satchel Vest rode up.

"Here! Here!" shouted the Colonel in a rage, "what are you doing, out of jail?"

"I'm minding my own business," returned Mace. "What are *you* doing out of jail?"

"I'll soon show you!" threatened Jones, reining his

blooded horse away and spurring off to find Mordecai Byrnes. But Satchel Vest Steen shoved his pistol to the front and stayed on, to watch the men.

"Look at the big fat stiff!" jeered Long Rope as he winked at Little Joe. "He's the Chief Chopping Block, or Dog Post, for Colonel Jones, of the Strychnine Outfit. Ain't he got a belly like a pisened pup? And look at that dodrammed vest!"

He turned away contemptuously and Little Joe spat in the dirt.

"I've heerd 'em say," he observed, "that them medals he wears was bought in a hock-shop, back East. But ain't he simply hell when he ketches some pore cowboy without the price of a meal? 'Meals Twenty-five Cents'—that's his motto, the danged hound. He ought to be shot twice at dawn!"

A crowd had swiftly gathered as Mace began his remarks; and when he threw back his head and laughed at Joe's sally the townspeople joined, to a man. There was nothing more thoroughly hated about the Hash-knife outfit than their charging for meals at the wagon. It violated all the principles of the old-time West, where every stranger was made welcome.

"You'd *have* to shoot him twice," jested Long Rope, "in order to get through his hide. Look at him set there, like he was going to do something! But *he* ain't bad—Uh—uh!"

He walked over brazenly and slapped Satchel Vest on the leg, as if he were handling a horse.

"Gee over!" he said, and laughed.

But behind his boyish laughter there was the memory of cruel hurts, when with hands tied behind him and his body bruised and sore, he had been led like a horsethief into town. And though Steen kept a bold front he was scared, for he saw Mace was hunting a fight. But his face was saved as Colonel Jones came galloping back, closely followed by Sheriff Byrnes.

"Now here!" began the Colonel, reining in his white stallion and pointing dramatically at Mace, "how does it happen, Mr. Byrnes, that this prisoner we brought in is at large and enjoying his liberty? I told you distinctly he was suspected of bank robbery, and under no circumstances to release him; and now I find him out, packing his horses to leave town—probably headed for the Mexican Line."

"Well, I'll tell you, Colonel," apologized Mordecai lamely, "you never brought in that bill. And even if you did, the mere possession of money is no crime. You've got to prove that it was stole. I couldn't hold him no longer."

"No!" spoke up Mace. "And another thing, Colonel—the sheriff here seen I was honest. I was too good a man to be kept in jail, so he up and let me go. But I'll be back, when the Grand Jury meets. So bring on your thousand dollar bill."

"Eh—eh! Honest!" blared Jones. "I could have you arrested on three counts. First you wrecked my blacksmith shop, then you stole a yearling—"

"And beat your cook out of two-bits!"

The high, malevolent voice of Little Joe cut in, heralding the Colonel's shame to the world; and as the guffaws of the populace came to his ears Jones turned on the sheriff in a pet.

"Arrest that man!" he said. "I'll swear out the warrant. And I want him locked up in jail."

"I don't know about that," observed Byrnes judiciously as he spied James G. Cramer hurrying up. "Several prominent citizens have gone on these boys' bonds—"

"And another thing!" shrilled Little Joe, "don't you git too danged brash or I'll swear out a few warrants, myself. I've been following your wagon, and I've got witnesses to prove that you brand every maverick you ketch. The little cowmen of this country are gitting good and tired and they have organized for protection, so you had better look out yourself or we'll throw *you* into the hoosegow."

This last was spoken on the inspiration of the moment, but it startled the Colonel out of his complacency. He paused and looked around at the unfriendly, alien faces, and Barfoot hopped in again.

"That goes for you, too!" he yapped at Steen. "You was there and running the wagon. So don't git so swelled up or we'll have you in jail and eating two meals a day."

The lordly Chief of Cowboys began to shrink and grow small before the withering blast of Joe's scorn and he turned his horse to go; but Breckenridge Jones was of a different breed and he paused to hurl back defiance.

"I've got one good case against you both," he cried, "and that is all I need. You were caught in the act while butchering one of my calves, and that hide is in the sheriff's safe."

He wheeled and spurred away while, loud and shrill, Little Joe hurled curses after him.

"I'll git you, you old billy goat!" he yelled. "You can't run no blazer on me!" And amid the plaudits of their friends the two horse-hunters rode forth to search for Whistling Rufus.

He was a horse better known than most of the people who inhabited the sparse region where he ranged. Wild Horse Mesa was his home, a long point in the high rim-rock that stretched south from the Guadalupe Mountains; but if pressed too hard he would leave the wooded mesa and take refuge in the desert to the south. Since a colt, he had wandered from desert lake to mountain spring, growing bigger and more wary from year to year until no rope or horse-trap would hold him.

He hurled himself against them with irresistible force or wheeled and fought his way out; and no man or gentle horse dared to stand before his charge—he came on with his snapping teeth bared. Ropes parted and fences broke, and many a mustanger went home nursing bruised knuckles and rope-burned hands. But every year they came back to match their guile against his, hoping at least to snare one of his colts.

Blooded mares had escaped their pastures to join his *manada* and bring forth long-legged colts; and with them, like protecting uncles, ran saddle-marked old range horses, rejoicing in their new-found freedom. Their manes and tails grew till they almost swept the ground—or waved like banners as, defiant of their masters, they broke through the lines and escaped. The man never lived who could gaze on their flight without a thrill of joy, but after they were gone a wild desire possessed him to catch Whistling Rufus and tame him.

What colts he would get if his proud spirit could be curbed to the confines of some strongly built pen! What race horses and nimble cutting-horses and iron-limbed mounts to ride dashing across mesa and plain!

"We're going to ketch him, this time," announced Little Joe confidently as they rode across the desert to the west. "That thousand dollar reward that Uncle Ben put up made all of his punchers hog wild. I built the finest corral you ever saw in your life—nine feet high and tied together the cables—but jest as the band was walking into the trap Ben's own boy, Sam, broke the line. He shook out a loop and charged in on Rufus, and the whole BH outfit follered. They tied to him, too, but he jerked Sam's saddle off and got away, ropes and all.

"Old Ben was so mad when he seen he was lost that he whaled them boys good with his *reata.* But the danged old walloper was in on it himself—that's why I quit and went home. Do you see all them trails, coming down off of the mountain right up at the mouth of Black Canyon? That's BH headquarters, but the wagon is over west, on the round-up."

Mace gazed at the washed-out trails, showing white among the bushes that clung to the limestone slope. It was a rough and jagged country, dry and barren of water except where deep canyons came out. One rim-rock after another divided the slope into terraces, which were studded with cedars and pinyons until, above high cliffs, the wooded heights appeared where the wild cattle and mustangs ran. But Little Joe kept west, skirting the base of the Guadalupes, until Wild Horse Mesa rose before them.

From the distance it looked like a long line of white bluffs breaking away from the black, timbered heights; but as they circled its point into the wide valley beyond a gap appeared in the rim.

"That's Jump Off Trail," explained Barfoot, "where the broom-tails come down for water. There's a big spring, right out on the flat. I built my trap over against that far hill, where we could drive them in after they'd drank; but, believe me or not, Whistling Rufus wouldn't drink, and he'd been without for three days. We could've caught all his mares—they were too pot-bellied to run—but we measured fifteen feet between his tracks, where he left there. He was hitting the wind like an antelope, and dragging Sam's saddle, to boot."

"Some horse, some horse!" observed Bowman regretfully. "Did Hockaday ever get back his saddle?"

"Tore to nothing over the rocks before his twine parted. That broke Sam of sucking eggs. And about a month later, when I seen Whistling Rufus, he still had a rope around his neck. Was he wild! Say, you ought to've heard him whistle! It sounded like a big bull elk!"

"That's what's spoiled him," opined Mace, who had lost a few ropes on bronks. "He's educated now and he knows we can't hold him. How do you figure on ketching him, Joe?"

"It's dead easy," grumbled Barfoot, "if they'll only do it. That's the only trail off of the mesa, for fifteen miles on both sides. But if you crowd them too hard they'll jump off anywhere, no matter if they do git killed. Now all we have to do is git a long line of cowboys and drive them horses down towards the point. You don't need to run 'em—jest keep 'em from water by stationing one man in this gap. Then in three or four days let the herd come down and drink and drive 'em easy inside the wings. But every time we try it some wart-head like Sam breaks the line and stampedes the bunch."

He heaved a heavy sigh over the weakness of all cowboys and reined Punkin out of the trail.

"No horse-sign," he said. "But we're close to the spring. No shod tracks, either, so they ain't been run lately. We'll keep out of sight and watch and maybe old Rufus will come down. They say a horse don't notice tracks, jest goes by smell, but you walk down one of these trails and leave a row of boot-tracks and Rufus will quit the country. That's how careful we have to be."

He edged in slowly until he sighted the spring. Then, just at dusk, they rode in and watered their horses, but only cattle had been at the spring.

"I can't understand this," murmured Barfoot uneasily, as he studied the tracks in the mud. "Here's some old, old horse-tracks, but they ain't been here lately. Sure hope they haven't left the country."

They camped that night within the gate of the big corral which had been built the year before. Heavy trees had been felled against the base of the wooded hill to form an impenetrable wall, and then against its flank two corrals had been constructed out of double cedar posts and peeled logs. Along the top of the main corral an inch-cable from an old mine had been stretched from post to post to withstand the greatest strain. The gate was set in rock, with a heavy spring to slam it shut and a trigger connected with the rope. All was ready for the rush which would test it to its utmost strength, but no mustang had ever entered the gate.

There was something almost spooky about the untrampled grass that had grown up inside the corral. Not even the range cattle had ventured down the lane which was formed by the mile-long wings. It was a pocket and the cows were afraid of it. But Mace saw that in a drive the pen would hold a herd of horses, no matter how madly they rushed.

At daylight they rode back to Cedar Spring, but not a single horse had come down.

"They've left," decided Joe, after cutting sign across Jump Off Trail. "Some rascal has been in here chasing them. Well, you go along the cliff as far as you can get and I'll ride down to Whisky Lake. That's out on the desert twenty miles or so—I'll meet you at the corral before dark."

He reined away muttering, for to lose the horses now would spoil all his plans for a drive; and Mace, well-content to ride by himself, jogged along the trail to the north. It followed the base of the broken and terraced cliff which formed the western rim of Wild Horse Mesa; a broad trail, but little traveled except by half-wild cattle, who took to the brush like deer. The sun was high above him when, crossing a side canyon, he cut the trail of horses, going up.

Long Rope stopped and leaned down to study the tracks in the white dust, then he turned and followed slowly up the wash. There were the dainty tracks of little colts, the broad imprints of mares and fillies and, overlaying them all as he came along last, the firm, round tracks of a stud. He was driving his little family before him and the trail seemed to lead to the top. But Joe had said that Jump Off Trail was the only path down from the mesa.

Within the walls of the narrow canyon the noonday sun beat down until the dead air was palpitant with heat. A few chipmunks and ground squirrels scuttled away over the hot rocks but all Nature seemed sunk in sleep. Even Brown Jug dropped his head as he mogged along, with the pack animal close behind, but as he rounded a point he woke up with a start, swiveling his ears and snuffing the air. Then, beneath an overhanging rock, a dozen forms came to life and Mace took down his rope with a jerk.

The canyon had come to an end and in the open space before him a blood-red stallion stood at bay. Mares and colts rushed about, seeking wildly to escape even up the terraced face of the cliff, but the stud held his ground as he stared. Then, swelling his glossy sides, he blew out his breath in a shrill whistle. Mace shook out his loop and turned the pack animal loose—he had trapped Whistling Rufus, himself!

There was the long, flowing mane, the tail that swept the ground, the blood-bay coat of the Steel-dusts. He was the king of all mustangs and Long Rope felt of his girth to see if his saddle would hold. Then he stepped down swiftly to give a jerk at his cinch, and in that instant the wild horse charged. Mace swung up on Brown Jug as he gave the stud the trail, and whirled his rope once for the throw. But that whirl was one too many. At sight of the loop Rufus stopped in his tracks and turned his head to the cliff.

It was high, almost vertical, but he ran madly at it with a last resounding whistle of alarm. Up the first slope he thundered, striking smoke from the rocks where the floodwaters had washed a way down; and behind him, never waiting, hurtled mare and filly and colt in a last wild attempt to escape. A cloud of dust rose up, through which as in a dream Mace beheld rocks kicked back, horses falling and scrambling up, getting a toe-hold and struggling on. Their front feet clung desperately while their scrabbling hind-legs heaved them up from lcdgc to lcdgc. Hc whirled his loop, waiting expectantly for Whistling Rufus to come tumbling within reach of his rope; but he fought his way up over the rim and the grunting mares followed close. Even the last, whinnying colt rimmed out, taking the cliff like a mountain sheep.

A cascade of rocks came bouncing down the cliff and Mace snapped back his loop in disgust.

"Well, I'll be damned!" he said at last, and rode back to report to Joe.

CHAPTER IX WILD HORSE MESA

IN the presence of Whistling Rufus—watching his desperate charge and his still more desperate flight—Long Rope had sat stunned by the fury of his going and the reckless devotion of his band. They had swarmed up the cliff like a waterfall flowing backward, defying all the laws of Nature; and when he waited for gravitation to hurl them back from the heights they had rimmed out and gained the mesa unhurt.

But what would have happened if, alone and unaided, he had tied to the charging stud? Another good saddle would have been scuffed over the rocks, another good horse jerked down, and the pride of one more puncher would have been dragged in the dust as he picked himself out of the dirt.

With a contrite and humble spirit Mace rode back to

the pen and reported his discovery to Joe. He even admitted that, when he tried to rope Rufus, he felt like a little child. But the hard-bitten Indian face of Joe Barfoot grew grimmer and he slapped his leg with his quirt.

"Right here," he said, "is where we ketch old Rufus, before he gits out of the country. I shore thought he was gone when I rode in to Whisky Lake and found them horses had pulled out. Too many of these would-be mustangers—I'm going over to see Ben in the morning."

They started back at dawn, after flagging Jump Off Trail to keep the wild horses from coming down; but it was almost noon before they found the BH wagon, and even then all the riders were gone. A band of Comanche bucks, relatives of Hockaday's Indian wife, sat stolidly in the shade of their ponies; the cook had a big meal all cooked; but only the distant yells of cowboys on the heights marked the slow return of the herd.

Then, over the rim of the upper bench, the first steers came racing towards the cutting-grounds on the edge of the plains. Anxious cows followed after them, mooing loudly for their calves that were dodging about in the ruck; and as they reached the parade-ground Ben Hockaday and Sam spurred down to hold them up. The great circle closed in, driving out cattle from every wash, and as the outlaws came trotting down, heads up for a break, every man at the wagon took to horse.

Through the hold-up herd these wild steers from the high mountains came boring their way with prodding horns. They paused as they broke out into the open again and saw the galloping horsemen before them, but while the foremost halted doubtfully and looked around, a huge brindle steer plunged on. Even among the mountain cattle he stood out like a giant; his massive head bowed down by the weight of his sweeping horns, his shoulders humped with age.

"Thar goes Old Brindle!" yelled Ben Hockaday, as the steer made a break for the hills. "Turn him back, boys! Rope him! Throw him! He's the best steer we've got fur that Rodeo!" And with a thunder of hoofs they were off.

The tall, half-Indian son of the burly old cowman whipped in and made his throw; but his rope slipped off of one long, tossing horn and Uncle Ben slapped on his loop. Joe and Mace galloped up as the rope came taut, and then Old Brindle charged. Hockaday's horse knew what was coming and left there like a bat, the rope parted and still he ran on—for close behind him with a heart-stilling blat the old outlaw was coming, horns down.

Joe roped at him and missed, the Comanches turned and fled, but as Brindle popped his tail and broke for the hills again, Brown Jug dashed resolutely in. Mace swung his long rope, rose in the stirrups and shot it forth, and the loop seemed to reach out like a hand. It curled up in front, settled down over both horns and was jerked tight with a mighty tug. Like an angler who feels the strike, Brown Jug leapt to one side and set his feet for the snub; and as the steer, yanked over backwards, hit the earth with a thud Mace Bowman went down the rope.

Yelling cowboys dashed in as with a magic all his own he grabbed up one hind leg, pushed it forward with his knee and lashed it to the two front feet. He took two quick dallies, threw a neat half-hitch, and threw up his hands from habit. The brindle steer was tied.

"Good boy!" cheered Old Ben. "By grab, a real champeen! Whar did *you* learn to throw a rope?"

"I'm from Túcumcari!" grinned Mace as he threw off his loop and swung gracefully up on Jug. "That's the way we tie to 'em, over there." And then as another outlaw came hightailing it for the hills he whipped out and tied to him. Again with effortless ease he slid out of his padded saddle while Brown Jug jerked the steer on his back, and as he crossed three legs and tied them hard and fast the BH boys gave a cheer.

"Sa-ay, boy, that's some hawse!" praised Sam Hockaday, as the first rush of outlaws was checked. "You ought to win first money, on him."

"The best rope-horse in New Mexico!" pronounced Mace. "He's got more sense than some men—Haven't you, Pet?" And Brown Jug snorted proudly, as if he had sensed the praise.

"Well, we're getting the steers!" boasted Sam exultantly. "They's three more jest like him, up thar in the timber, tied down to lct 'em cool off. Regular cedar-brake moss-heads, with horns about six feet across. Did you find old Whistling Rufus?"

"He's up on the mesa, right now!" broke in Joe, as Ben Hockaday and the rest rode up. "So any time you want to, Uncle Ben, you can start that wild horse drive."

"You don't say!" exclaimed Hockaday, his eyes gleaming avidly. "This is playing right into my hand. Hyar's two of my wife's people, from up on the Palo Duro, that know how to walk 'em down."

He turned to his long-haired relations and talked rapidly in Comanche, with a lot of sign-language thrown in.

"He says 'Yes'!" he said at last, as the old chief grunted. "They can walk 'cm down in four days. All he asks of us is to hold them on the mesa. Him and his boy will do the rest. I told him I'd give him the pick of the fillies if they'd put the bunch in the pen."

"Good enough!" agreed Little Joe. "But you tell him to be careful. My pardner here jumped thcm yesterday in that blind canyon above Sand Tanks and they climbed plumb over the rim."

"Up the cliff?" marveled Hockaday. "That's Whistling Rufus! We've got to wear him down, boys, or he'll never be took alive. Don't none of you ever crowd him or he'll jump right off the mesa, and take the whole band with him. Well, we'll brand up our calves and turn the rest loose. I'm afeerd Rufe will leave the country."

He gave rapid orders and, hardly stopping to eat, his cowboys changed horses and rushed through the work of branding. Then, changing again, they took the trail up the mountain to cut off every avenue of escape. The round-up was abandoned, the town-herd sent to the ranch and, each man on his best mount, they set out to catch Whistling Rufus. But though they all rode like mad there was none of them half so wild as Old Ben.

"I'm going to ketch that thar hawse," he announced to Mace and Joe, "if it's the last act of my misspent life. And the first man that ropes at him or skeers him in any way—that rascal walks back to town. My wife's brother, Ossa-keep, knows jest how to handle 'em—he never gits off a walk. Keep 'em moving—that's his motto—and after three or four days, drive 'em down and let 'em drink. Then, while they're pot-bellied, work 'em into the corral. But no hawses, mind ye! On foot!"

"You don't need to talk to *me!*" retorted Little Joe, bitterly. "I reckon I know my job. And you be careful I don't ketch *you* out there, swinging a Mother Hubbard loop and skeering 'em into fits."

"Never mind!" grumbled Hockaday, ignoring the reference, "I ain't kicking, mind you, I'm jest *telling* you! And I reckon I've got a right to say my mind—ain't I turned my round-up loose? Who ever heerd of a cowman doing that, jest to ketch a passel of bronks? But I'm never going to rest in peace until I put my rope on Rufe!"

He spurred on ahead, burning up with anxiety, throwing his circle farther and farther west; until at last, just at dusk, they sighted Whistling Rufus with his tail up like a flag. He was trotting across the mesa, driving his big herd of mares before him, and Hockaday gave a yell.

"Thar he goes, boys!" he hollered. "Now line out from cliff to cliff and cut 'em off down thar at the Neck. Joe, you keep out of sight and ride fur Jump Off Trail—and don't you let him through! Understand? Build a big, strong fence, and take your pardner with you. And be keerful, boys! Be-e keer-ful!"

Mace and Joe rode off in the gathering gloom and the next morning as they worked at the head of Jump Off Trail they saw the herd come by. A big, sorrel mare with LC on her hip was in the lead of the galloping band and in the rear came Whistling Rufus, his head and tail up, whistling loudly at every breath. He was driving them hard, looking back over his shoulder; but not for a full hour did old Ossa-keep appear, following stolidly along on their trail.

He was stripped down to his moccasins and G-string, with a wicker water-bottle and a sack of pinole slung over his shoulder. They came by again towards evening, the horses on a trot, gazing wistfully towards Jump Off Trail. They were thirsty now, after a long day of running, and some old horses were lagging behind. But in the rear Whistling Rufus still looked back over his shoulder, and far to the south there walked a man. It was Ossa-keep's son, stepping free in his trim moccasins; and he too carried a bottle and sack.

The next day the herd dashed in from the north, the old mare still in the lead, but at sight of the two men at the head of the trail they halted and stood at gaze. Then, whistling angrily, the stud circled his band and trotted out to look. But hardly had he approached this closed door that led to freedom, when he wheeled and went galloping back. Squealing and biting, he rounded up his *manada* and drove them savagely on; and soon, not a quarter-mile behind, old Ossa-keep came striding along.

After their first short run the herd slowed down and stopped, the older horses in the drag; but behind them like a Nemesis the Indian followed close, and they leapt up and scampered ahead. In and out among the cedars they fled in a great circle; avoiding the line of horsemen that stretched across the Neck, turning fretfully on their tireless pursuers. But wherever they went the Indians kept on their trail, and on the third day they had dropped to a walk.

They plodded by with heads down, their flanks gaunted for lack of water, while not a hundred yards behind them and still going strong, old Ossa-keep herded them along. So spent were they and leg-weary that they moved like automatons, following hopelessly along the same old trail; but each time they approached Jump Off the stallion came closer, whistling defiantly, his eyes red with rage.

"That old fighting fool is going to charge right

through here," predicted Mace as they ran for their mounts; but at sight of the two men on horseback Whistling Rufus turned and fled. That was the one fear left him, though he plodded on morosely a few paces ahead of Ossa-keep. He had felt the bite of whistling ropes and the shock as strange horsemen jerked him down; but at dawn of the fourth day, when the Indians began to crowd him, he turned and chased them back.

Ossa-keep returned on his tough Indian pony, his son caught up his mount; and then over the fifteen miles of mesa they pushed the jaded herd on. Other horsemen came and went, from the Neck to Jump Off Trail, for Uncle Ben Hockaday was in a fever of excitement as the time to make the run approached. For three days and three nights the horses had been on the move, and the feed on the mesa was dry; but though hunger and thirst had broken their spirit Ossa-keep kept relentlessly after them. Four days—four nights—he said, using his sign-talk. They would let them drink at dawn.

As the first light appeared Mace helped tear down the fence and retreated to the valley below. The cowboys were spread out in two rows, forming a line from the gap to the wings; and shortly after sunup the frantic herd came plunging down and rushed to the spring to drink. Ossa-keep and his son remained up on the trail, where they could watch every move that they made, and not until Rufus had drunk his fill did the old man start down toward them. He walked slowly, just as for four days and four nights he had plodded along on their trail, and the waterlogged mustangs ignored him. Only Whistling Rufus and the LC mare turned to follow him with glassy eyes.

The Indian drew near, he was almost upon them, when with a sudden whistle of alarm Rufus roused up and circled his band. He turned on his pursuer, his teeth skinned wickedly; then, snapping and biting, he rounded up the herd and took the trail to the north. But as they headed up the valley a line of horsemen appeared and they swung back, breaking into a trot. But other riders rose before them, blocking their way to the south, and with a flirt they hurtled off to the west.

They were inside the brush wing the first rush, and the Comanche beckoned the cowboys to close in. Then he walked along behind, never crowding them as they went up the trail, and they kept on until they sighted the gate. It stood open, its posts hidden behind two green trees, but the LC mare knew traps.

She stopped short and snorted, Whistling Rufus rushed up; but just as he was starting his *manada* out, Ben Hockaday and his cowboys charged. They came thundering up the lane, whooping and yelling and swinging their ropes, and the mustangs broke and fled. Past the two green trees with the posts behind, a big corral opened up, too high for the best of them to jump; but Whistling Rufus made a run and smashed against the fence, and the rest came pouring in.

There was a succession of terrific crashes as one

after the other the frantic broom-tails hit the corral. But it held, and from his hiding-place Little Joe pulled the rope and the great gate swung shut and latched.

"We've got 'em!" yelled Ben Hockaday, climbing recklessly up the gate. And the cowboys whooped for joy.

CHAPTER X THE MAN-EATERS

IN such a simple way, after balking them for years, was Whistling Rufus caught. The load of water in his belly weighed the game stallion down—his great thirst had betrayed him at last. With his frantic mares and colts running in every direction, skinning and bruising their heads against the poles, he made one jump to scrabble up over the logs and fell back, sullen and beaten.

With exultant whoops the cowboys topped the fence, looking down on the milling herd; and as each fear-mad mustang threw her weight against the corral they laughed and fanned her back. Then an inside gate opened and, one after the other, they let the mares and colts into the roping pen. It was smaller and stouter, with a snubbing-post in the center, and as the wild horses quieted down a puncher walked in, dragging his loop out of sight behind.

It shot out with snake-like swiftness as a mare darted past. The loop, turning up, snared the flashing front feet, jerked taut—and she hit the ground. When she rose up, half-stunned, the rope was snubbed around the post and the first jump she made she went down again. Another rope came flying and lassed her hind feet and the wild creature was in their power. Soon a tie-rope was knotted in the long hair of her tail and fastened to one forefoot. After that she could walk, on three legs, but at the first leap to run she went down.

Ossa-keep and his son took their pick of the blooded fillies which had fallen a victim to their wiles, but the ten worst fighters among the big band of mares were set aside for the Rodeo. But with these wild creatures to ride and the mountain steers to rope, it would be a Rodeo no longer. The El Toro carnival would be Pioneer Day, and no one but cowhands need apply. There was a hereafter coming for Tex McMullen and all his kind, unless they had worked in the hills. Every man who rode a bronk would have to saddle him in the open—the chutes would be torn down.

Long into the day the battle went on as man after man took his turn in the roping-pen, tying down mares and fillies and colts. But at last Whistling Rufus was left alone in the big corral and Ben Hockaday shook out his rope.

"Now open up that gate!" he shouted, "and watch me tie to Rufe."

"You better go easy!" shrilled Little Joe as the old cattleman built a big loop. "Let Sam come in and help!"

"When I need any help—or any advice from you—I'll ask for it!" announced Uncle Ben.

He rode in confidently on his big, rawboned roan, and Whistling Rufus snorted and wheeled. Then he turned to the fence as if about to leap and a warning yell went up. But Hockaday only grinned, spurring in as he swung his rope, and Rufus crouched like a cat. First he looked at the fence, then he turned towards the gate, and Uncle Ben made a throw.

Every man on the fence saw that the loop was too big—and few indeed can rope a horse standing still. As it left Hockaday's hand Whistling Rufus made a bolt and the rough strands barely grazed his rump. But at the feel of the rope he kicked out like a flash and headed, pell-mell, for the gate. Two cowboys who straddled its top let go all holds and fell. There was a shout, and he mounted up like a bird. But the high crosspiece stopped him and he came tumbling back, to land on his feet in the corral.

For a moment with tumbled mane and eyes that glowed like fire Whistling Rufus stood and glared. Then he charged the whole length of the wide corral and hurled himself at the high back fence. It was a magnificent leap and he clung like a cat as he came down across the top log. His hind feet kicked him over, falling headlong in a smashing somersault, and he landed with a crash—outside!

There was a rush for the fence, to see where he had gone, and as the cowboys scrambled up Rufus rose and trotted away, looking back over his shoulder proudly. He held his tail high, like a blood-red flag, and at every step he reached out farther. Half an hour later he was a streak of dust across the desert and Ben Hockaday was still cursing his luck.

"Heh! What did I tell you?" railed Little Joe, heartlessly. "And talk about your Mother Hubbard loops! You've spoiled him now—they's no fence will hold him. Why the hell didn't you wait for Sam?"

"Well, let him go!" apostrophized Uncle Ben, shaking his fist at the point of dust. "He's the orneriest old fence-breaker in New Mexico and I wouldn't have him, nohow. We've got his mares and colts—and we'll keep 'em, too—but the fust thing he'd do would be to bust down the gate and turn the whole passel loose."

"That's right," agreed Mace, as the other boys winked. "And any one of them little colts may grow up to be another Rufus."

"No, suh!" flared back Hockaday, changing his ground again. "There'll never be another Whistling Rufus. But I've changed my mind—didn't want the rascal, nohow. The fust man that ketches him kin have him."

"Well, come on!" blared big Sam, giving his father a black look. "Let's drive what we've caught back home. Swing that gate open, boys, and let 'em come out; and if any get loose, tie to 'em!"

The massive gate was flung open, the mares came limping out, falling flat every time they ran; and so, a sorry procession, they crippled and floundered across the desert until they reached the BH ranch, after dark. There they were penned until morning in the big pole corral that stood at the mouth of the canyon, and the next day, one by one, they were released from their tie-ropes and turned into the Black Canyon pasture.

Walls a thousand feet high cut them off on both sides, the narrow entrance was blockaded like a fort, and not even a Whistling Rufus could escape up the canyon, so baffling were the potholes and waterfalls. The only way out was through the gate at the mouth and it was reinforced and bound fast with rawhide. Then, to keep the mustangs from hurling themselves against it, a huge bull-hide was hung across.

"Thar!" pronounced Uncle Ben as he stood off and surveyed his work, "them broom-tails are caught to stay caught. The hawse or cow never lived that could stand a rattling cowhide. They'll be thar when we come back."

He rode off with all his men to resume his neglected round-up, and while Mace stood guard Little Joe went to town to notify the Rodeo Committee. They had the bronks and steers to put on a Pioneer Day from which El Toro would date time. The only question was—could *any* man rope or ride them? And could they be delivered alive?

Three days before the contest the BH wagons came rumbling back from El Toro. The round-up was over, the beef-herd sold and shipped, and the cowboys were feeling glorious. After combing the Guadalupes from the summit to the desert, fighting bronks, roping moss-heads and standing guard, they felt that the taming of a few outlaw horses was nothing but child's play. They got in early and after a couple more drinks brought the mustangs down to the pen.

Ropes flew and horses stampeded as one by one the worst were dragged out; and then, in the round corral, Sam Hockaday climbed the LC mare. Little Elsie was the name which the facetious Committee had given to this mountain of man-eating hate, and as Sam pulled up the blinder and raked her with his spurs she swelled up like a toy balloon. Then she crouched like a cat and jumped high, with a writhing twist that changed her end for end in the air. She came down bawling, jumped again and sank so low that his long legs were knocked out of the stirrups. The next thing Sam knew he had landed on his head and she was cow-kicking around the corral.

"She'll do!" they shouted gleefully and led out a big dun with tiger stripes down her back.

"I'll ride her!" yelped Wash, Sam's younger brother. And Seven Rivers threw him a mile.

"Two!" they counted; and at the end of the Saturnalia ten man-eating bronks were off in a pen by themselves.

There was no necessity of trying out the steers, as every old moss-head had put up a battle when they brought them down from the brakes. Some had horns six feet across and stood higher than a horse, with a homicidal stare in their eyes, so the best were roped and thrown and their front feet tied up for the long drive into town. The next evening the BH chuck-wagon came rumbling into El Toro and unhooked outside Pioneer Park, and just before dark the two herds of contest animals were brought in and safely penned. Then the boys went to town to celebrate in advance—and bet their wages that the Hash-knives would lose.

CHAPTER XI LITTLE EVA

THE broad street of El Toro was swarming with people and horsemen in gala attire, and the saloons were crowded to the doors. Old friends met on every corner, and to celebrate the occasion the bar-keepers were kept on the run. In the Long Horn Saloon, James G. Cramer, the genial mixer, was serving drinks and taking money with both hands; but he stopped in the midst of a highball when Mace Bowman and Little Joe pushed in.

"Well, well!" he exclaimed, beckoning them up to the bar, "this calls for the drinks on the house. Gentlemen all, drink to the health of our two champion ropers—Joe Barfoot and Mace Bowman, of Túcumcari."

He scattered glasses down the bar with a dexterous flip and set out the big, black bottles.

"Here's luck to our friends," he proposed, raising his glass, "and confusion to the Hash-knives. Did you get some wild horses, boys?"

"Regular man-eaters!" confided Mace. "They're too

dam' rank for me. You can't rope, after you've topped one of them."

"No?" observed Cramer, smiling wisely. "That's rather unfortunate for Tex. We've placed the bronk-riding first."

"Yes, and listen," interposed Red Tutlow, speaking hoarsely in Bowman's ear, "we're going to give him Little Elsie."

"Nope—make it Seven Rivers," suggested Mace. "I want to beat him at roping first, and Little Elsie will bust him wide open."

"Well, Seven Rivers, then," agreed Red, reluctantly. "That is, if I don't change my mind. You're sure you're going to win?"

"Feeling lucky as a fool!" asserted Long Rope.

"Then I'll tell you what I'll do," proposed Tutlow. "You go back and get some sleep and lay off of this booze and I'll give him Seven Rivers."

"But I rope better when I'm drunk!" objected Mace.

"Yes, I know," nodded Red. "That's what they all say. But you can't talk to me—I'm the Champion Booze Fighter of New Mexico."

"Well—all right," grumbled Long Rope and, taking Joe with him, he rode back to the BH wagon.

"What's the matter?" asked the cook. "Have a fight?"

"Nope, we're barred," returned Mace, jerking his bedroll off the pile. "Might as well get a little shut-eye."

"Sure! Sure!" agreed the cook. "But say, boys, do

me a favor. Watch the wagon while I git me a bottle."

"Go ahead and git drunk!" spoke up Little Joe, magnanimously. "But don't you bring back no bottle. We're contestants, see? We got to be careful. One drink would spoil his nerve!"

"Whose nerve?" demanded Long Rope. "I could drink a quart of whisky and—"

"Yes, but I notice," cut in Joe, "that Colonel Jones savvies his business. He keeps them professionals out of town. He knows they cain't drink and win. And when Eva comes in, do you want to be drunk? She thinks you and me are gentlemen!"

"Well, have it your own way," sighed Mace, stretch. ing out. "You don't reckon she'll give us a kiss?"

"Us!" echoed Barfoot. "What the hell are you talking about? Little Eva don't kiss nobody!"

"No?" returned Long Rope. "Well, she shore kissed me when I throwed Gilhooly into the lake."

"You're drunk!" accused Joe. "That was only an anvil. And what give you the idee that was a lake?"

"Yes, and I suppose," railed Mace, "I never even whipped him? You shut up, now, and go to sleep!"

"Huh!" grunted Barfoot. "Jest listening to old Cramer makes you believe everything he says. You think you took Gilhooly and tied him to his anvil and sunk him in the Bottomless Spring. But I'm here to tell you you never did no sech thing—and she never kissed you, neither!"

"Aw, you're jealous!" scoffed Long Rope. "Lay down and go to sleep. I'm not trying to steal your girl."

"No—because you cain't do it," answered Little Joe, and from arguing they dropped off to sleep.

But in the morning, much refreshed, their petty bickerings were forgotten and they turned out a calf to practice on. Out of courtesy, Joe Barfoot had not entered in the steer-tying contest, and Mace had not entered the calf-tying. As pardners they did not wish to be pitted against each other—and the steers were too big for Joe. He did not have the weight nor the strength to throw them, but at calf-roping he was as good as the best. His yellow horse, Punkin, was steady and sure, and Barfoot never missed a throw. But Bowman was saving Jug for the battle with the steers and only warmed him up and withdrew.

He was lying on his bed in the shade of the wagon, brooding idly on the events of the day, when with the blare of a French horn a Concord stage hove in sight and he saw Colonel Jones on the seat. The six horses were extended in a Wild West gallop, a swarm of cowboys loped on both sides; while in the rear, popping his whip, came Sowbelly Johnson, every pan in his chuck-wagon jangling. From force of habit, as the small boys gave a whoop, the Colonel rose and doffed his white hat; but Long Rope never moved from his comfortable bed as the Hash-knife outfit dashed by. They were no friends of his, and in the lead of the cowboys rode Satchel Vest and Tex McMullen.

But what horses they rode! What rigging they had! Every animal pranced and champed, their saddles gleamed with silver; and in the remuda trotted Scrambled Eggs. He was Tex McMullen's rope-horse—a beautiful chestnut, with quick knees and wide-set eyes—too good a horse for a mucker like Tex. He had won him the championship of the world. Long Rope eyed him and sighed, ignoring the fleeting glances of the show-riders as they passed. They were welcome to their rigging, their beaver hats and angora shaps—but Bowman loved a good horse.

The BH boys had been up late the evening before and some of them still slept in the shade, but at the clatter of hoofs and the rumble of wagons they roused up from their dreams to stare.

"All drunk," observed McMullen, glancing down at them disdainfully; and Sam Hockaday jeered back as they passed.

"Jest wait till you see them bucking-hawses," he said, *sotto voce.* "Then *we'll* have a chance to laugh."

The Hash-knives parked their wagons farther down the fence, away from other outfits, but as soon as their triumphal entry was over the cowboys wheeled and rode back. A crowd of boys by the cattle corral caught their eyes and they reined in and looked over the fence.

"What the devil!" barked McMullen, as he glimpsed the long-horned steers; and Sam Hockaday made a noise like escaping steam. It came in handy while shoving dogies through the chutes, but Tex knew it was intended for him.

"Aw, phooey!" he called back; and then as he looked further his eyes fell on the corralful of bronks. One glance was enough to tell the whole story—they were wild horses, straight off the range.

"A-aw—cripes!" he protested, turning to ride back to the Colonel, "them's nothing but broom-tail mares!"

"What's the matter?" yelled Sam, "can't you ride 'em?"

"You're trying to do us dirt!" accused McMullen, heatedly. "You know you can't win so you've shipped in these outlaws. I'm going to protest to the Committee!"

"Too-oo bad!" mocked Hockaday. "You must think we give a dam' whether you ride or set in the stands. They ain't too bad fur us—*we* can top 'em."

"I don't have to git killed jest to give you a laugh!" flung back Tex as he galloped off. And once more, like the sizz of an overheated engine, Sam Hockaday let off steam.

Colonel Jones cantered over, all buckskin and high boots, and examined the animals in the pens. Then with his cowboys behind him he rode back to town and returned with Monroe and Red Tutlow.

"I protest," he began, "against this obvious effort to discriminate against Western Shows. I have in my employ the finest cowboys in the world, the picked men from all over the great West; but if these steers and horses are used in the contests I must withdraw every man. We are about to begin our fourth successful season, our great triumphal march from contest to contest, depicting to the people the glorious deeds of the Old West while my men compete with all comers. But, rather than have my horses gored and my best riders injured, I must decline to participate in this contest."

"Huh! Them steers are all right!" roared Uncle Ben Hockaday, who had followed the protestants from town. "We picked 'em up on our regular round-up. They've all been roped and thrown. And every hawse in that corral has been tried out by my own sons. That shows that they kin be rode!"

"They're all mares!" roared back Satchel Vest. "We know all about them. Those are wild horses—right off the range."

"Well, what do you want?" retorted Hockaday scathingly. "Trick hawses, that's ben worked twice a day? Hawses that won't pitch at all without a bucking-strap cinched across their flanks? This ain't a circus—it's Pioneer Day—and you don't need to compete if you're skeered!"

"It is easy to see," observed Jones to the Committee, "that my men are being discriminated against. But if these sagebrush cowboys think they can keep us from competing, all I will say is, they're badly mistaken. I have in Western Shows the finest aggregation of ropers and riders that have ever been assembled in one band, every man a real product of the West. And if they wish to go in and demonstrate their superiority I believe they will win every event. But before I give my consent I want to see one of those horses rode."

"You'll see that this afternoon," responded Neil

Monroe. "That is, if you attend our performance. But if you don't attend I can assure you, right now, that your presence will never be missed. We were giving these Pioneer Day contests before you came into the country—"

"That's it," broke in the Colonel. "That shows you're jealous. You're trying to keep the prize money in town. But under the law we are entitled—"

They were still arguing back and forth while Mace Bowman, unperturbed, took his ease by the deserted wagon, when a vision in white came trotting gayly by, and he looked up to behold Little Eva. She was riding her white pony and at sight of the rough cowboy she reined in and blushed as she bowed.

"How do you do, Mr. Long Rope!" she greeted. "Are you resting up for the afternoon?"

"Well, howdy do!" exclaimed Mace, scrambling up and returning her bow. "No, it makes me so tired, hearing them Hash-knife boys yammer, I had to lay down and rest."

"Do you feel strong enough, then," she inquired archly, "to shake hands with a Hash-knife girl?"

"Why, sure!" he answered bluffly, taking her lily-white hand. "I reckon you and me can be friends."

"Oh, I hope so!" she responded with a sigh. "Don't you know," she went on, smiling wistfully, "I feel that I know you real well. Only, of course, I've only seen you once. Is your eye all right? It looks red."

"That comes from looking at Tex McMullen," he explained, and she burst into a merry laugh.

"You're such a funny man!" she exclaimed. "I never laughed so much in my life as when you threw that big anvil into the spring. And Dad thought it was Martin Gilhooly!"

She glanced at her father to see if she was observed, and fixed him with coquettish blue eyes.

"Mr. Gilhooly," she confided, "is beating his wife again and acting like a regular Bluebeard, so next time you're going by stop in and make us a call."

"Yeah—thanks," he returned, suddenly grim. "That'll all depend on whether I get sent up for stealing that Hash-knife calf."

"That's what I came to see you for," she confessed impulsively. "I'm so sorry you were hurt, and I know you just killed that calf to get a beefsteak to put on your eye. And of *course* you're not a bank robber! So anything I can do, let me know. I hope I'll see you again," she ended hurriedly; and Mace looked around to see Joe.

"Oh! How do you do!" she exclaimed, smiling roguishly as Joe sat tongue-tied. "Why don't you come and see me any more?"

"I—I— We been busy!" answered Barfoot lamely.

"I don't believe it!" she declared, winking the other eye at Mace. "Don't you think that's a poor excuse? Why, Mr. McMullen says he'd give a horse, any time, just to be where he could see me ride by!"

"Yes, he's a fine feller," spoke up Mace as Joe failed to make a come-back. "And I reckon he sees you right often."

"We-ell—sometimes," she admitted. "It gets lonely out there, with nobody riding by."

"Well, Joe will be along, pretty soon," promised Mace. And Little Eva showed both dimples in reply.

"Oh, will you?" she asked, turning to Joe. "We'll be going on the road, pretty soon."

"You bet ye!" responded Barfoot. "Say, your old man is hollering!" And Eva turned, suddenly pale.

"Come over here!" commanded the Colonel, who had been shouting unnoticed. He was angry, and she trotted off meekly. "You go back to your mother," he ordered. "No, come right along with me!"

Then as the cowboys stood at gaze he rode furiously away, while Little Eva took his dust.

"The old walloper!" cursed Little Joe. "He treats her like dirt." But Long Rope only laughed.

"She ain't suffering," he opined.

"He yaps her around like a dog!" grouched Joe. " 'Come here'—'Go home'! Wow, wow!"

"Aw, he's all right," answered Mace. "Just sore about them steers."

"No! He treats her like that all the time! She cain't go anywhere alone!"

"She's a mighty pretty girl," observed Bowman, philosophically. "Somebody has got to take care of her."

"But she came out to see me, all the same," grinned Joe. "And gimme hell for not coming to call. Say, you watch my smoke when I git into this calf-roping. I'm shore going to beat McMullen. Did you notice how she brought in his name?"

"She was just kind of hinting," nodded Mace, "that she'd like to see him took down."

"I'll take him down," promised Little Joe, vengefully. "I'll beat him, if he is a champeen."

"All right," agreed Mace. "And just to back your hand I'll take him down some, myself."

CHAPTER XII PIONEER DAY

THE Pioneer Day parade formed early, to lead the crowd out to the park, and the sidewalks were jammed with men. Long-bearded mountaineers and wolf-faced rustlers rubbed shoulders with stern-eyed cattlemen, for the word had gone out that the Hashknives were due to lose, and the back-country is strong on revenge. The year before, the Western Shows riders had carried off every prize—but now there was a new deal on.

In the lead on his big horse rode Neil Monroe, the President; and Red Tutlow, Arena Director and Manager. Then came James G. Cramer, magnificently arrayed, and Phat Noland, Champion Roughriding Barber. Behind them, huge and swarthy, loomed Ben Hockaday and his three sons, El Toro's main hope in the bucking contests; and, mingled with the BH cowboys, Joe Barfoot and Mace Bowman, each mounted on his well-trained rope-horse.

A band of Comanches with long braids and red blankets gave a final touch of color to the scene, but just as the procession moved slowly into town there was a clatter of hoofs from behind. Up the broad main street, with his cohorts behind him, came Colonel Jones on his beautiful white stud. He held his hat in his hand, his long curls swept his shoulders, and when the little boys cheered he bowed. Then genially, as if it were his due, he took his place at the head of the parade.

Every one of his men was superbly mounted, their saddles gleamed with first-prize plates; and as the band struck up, their horses pranced and champed, winding sidewise at sly touches of the spur. And what cowboys they were who bestrode them so masterfully—the pick of all the West—broad-shouldered and burly or slim and graceful, according to their events. But the crowd only gave them black looks, while the sagebrush cowboys who tagged along behind showed signs of open rebellion—until Ben Hockaday held up his hand.

"Let 'em lead, boys," he said. "We'll show 'em up later. Jest wait till the contests begin!"

The grandstand and bleachers of Pioneer Park were crowded to the top when the first big event was announced—the World's Championship Two Calf Roping Contest. From the corral at the end of the field a fast yearling was driven out. He trotted past the roper who sat his horse behind the deadline—his loop coiled and raised, his tie-rope between his teeth—rider and horse in a tremor to go.

The calf broke into a gallop at the thirty-foot line, the starter slapped down his flag; and then with a clatter of hoofs the cowboy took after him, chased and doubled and made his throw. But his loop was too big, the active calf leaped clear through it; and he followed angrily, building a new loop. There were two calves to be roped, but no man could expect to win unless he caught the first throw.

Another calf, and another, were hazed out of the corral and sent off to a running start; but not until Tex McMullen rode out on Scrambled Eggs did the grandstands rise and cheer. His calf was little and fast, a quick dodger and educated, but as he went prancing across the line Scrambled Eggs leapt into the air and landed running like the wind. He was off at a single jump; and Tex with his short, tied rope leaned forward and slapped on his loop. At a tug on the reins, Scrambled Eggs set his feet and stopped short. McMullen stepped off behind, snatching the hogging-string from his teeth, and went down his twine on the run. The little calf snapped over backwards and landed with a bump and Tex grabbed him before he could bounce. There was a tense moment of waiting as he looped the two forefeet, crossed a hind one and made his tie. Then he threw up his hands and laughed.

"Beat that!" he yelled back at the cowboys.

There were twenty mountain boys, sitting their horses behind the deadline and waiting their turn to rope; but none of them could beat Tex's time. Little Joe came the nearest, but he fell two seconds short and the contest closed for the day. On the morrow the ropers would compete again and the best average time would win.

The next event was a Cowboys' Relay Race and the Hash-knife riders won again. Their blooded race horses took the lead from the start and the grandstands and bleachers turned glum. But when Little Eva rode out on her rocking-horse pony and carried off first prize for Trick Riding they relented and gave her a cheer. That was circus stuff—they were waiting for the bronks.

With a bellowing squeal a wild broom-tail came dashing out and went the full length of the park. Grim mountain-boys closed in on her, choked her down with the hackamore and led her back in front of the stands. For this was Pioneer Day, and mounting in the chutes was barred. Dick Hockaday, the youngest and most reckless of them all, brought his saddle out and threw it down. They then grabbed Battle Axe by both ears and slipped a gunnysack over her eyes while the saddle was eased on and cinched.

Young Dick tried his stirrup and she cow-kicked at his foot. But he was watching and avoided the blow. He tried again and after the kick he swung quickly up into the saddle.

"Let 'er go!" he whooped, tightening his grip on the hackamore and jerking up the blind; and Battle Axe jumped straight up. She hogged up her back and came down with a savage grunt, spurning the ground as she leaped again. Then she went all to pieces and in a cloud of dust Dick Hockaday joined the birds.

"Eee-hooo!" shouted the cowboys, and the Roman holiday was on.

Horse after horse bucked and sunfished and swapped ends, cow-kicking at the spurs that roweled her flanks, baring her teeth as she reached back to bite. It was a battle from the start and the stands went wild as bronk after bronk flung her rider. But when big Sam Hockaday swung up on Oh Suzanna he rode her to a finish. There was no pistol-shot or whistle after the first twenty seconds, no pick-up men to save the worn rider—it was Pioneer Day and range conditions prevailed, and at last a mountain-man had won.

The general run of dudes from Western Shows had declined to participate in the massacre, but when the triumphant whoops of the audience had subsided, Tex McMullen strode out to defend his title. He clumped out grudgingly, wearing his heavy, winged shaps to protect his legs in a fall; but it was ride or lose his place in all the other contests, and Tex was out for the dough. As the last man to report he had drawn Seven Rivers, the big, tiger-striped dun that had outclassed them all but Little Elsie, and she was reserved for the finals.

"Put her over in the chute," pleaded McMullen, as Seven Rivers set back on the hackamore; but the hard-hearted Arena Director told the boys to drag her up and Tex clamped on his hull.

"You scoundrels are trying to kill me," he remarked, as he cinched up his belt and stepped on. "But I'll show you, by grab, I'm the champion yet. Let 'er go!" And he pulled up the blinder.

Seven Rivers did not wait. She had been topped once before and had got her man the first jump. She jumped again, high and wide, changing ends as she descended and landing with a devastating jar—but McMullen only hooked her in the neck. She swung in circles, bawling madly, she hopped up and down; but both spurs in the flanks finally broke her fit of bucking and Tex made a grandstand dismount. He threw up both feet and dropped off, waving his hat, and all the women cheered. He had made the best ride for the day.

But there were others yet to ride, and as the next bronk came out Tex sank down against the fence. He had had a terrible shaking up, and as he sat there Mace Bowman walked by. There was a Judas-faced smile on his twisted lips and he stopped with his hands on his hips.

"Pretty work!" he observed. "You put up a good ride. But what's the matter, Cowboy—you look kinder pale!"

McMullen opened his eyes slightly and muttered a curse.

"They jobbed me!" he complained. "I'm all shot to hell. The roughest dam' horse I ever rode."

"What—*her?*" laughed Mace, suddenly resuming his normal tone. "She ain't *nothing* to what they've got. You wait till you ride in the finals!"

Tex snapped his bleared eyes open and stared up at Bowman.

"Oh—you!" he grunted. "What the devil are you doing out of jail?"

"They just turned me loose to beat you in the steer-tying. And it looks like I had you beat. You couldn't rope a post with a Mother Hubbard loop, the way your tongue hangs out."

"Aw, shut up," snarled McMullen, "and leave me alone. I can beat you with one hand."

"You want to bet?" challenged Long Rope, bringing out a roll of bills. "I'll go you, for a thousand dollars!"

"Ahr, you and your phony bill!" scoffed Tex. "I haven't robbed any banks, myself."

"No, you haven't got the nerve to," came back Bowman. "And just wait till you see them *steers*. I'd like to have a dollar for every horse they've gored. We brought 'em down especially for you."

"You go to hell!" grumbled McMullen morosely; and Mace grinned back as he left.

"All right, Mister Champeen Everything!" he taunted. "We've got your hide hung on the fence."

He went back to the corral where the moss-heads were confined, walking fast and talking to himself. In spite of everything Tex McMullen had made good his boasts. He had won first place in calf-roping and bronk-riding, but could he tie down his steer? Mace swung his boot at a staggy-looking steer who hooked at it and charged the fence. He was as fierce or fiercer than Old Brindle.

"Keep that one for McMullen," he said to the corral-boss; and lined up with the cowboys at scratch.

The first steer to come out was a wild one, but a mountain-boy tied him down. Another one left the chutes and a second boy took after him, while the crowd in the grandstands cheered. Here at last was an event where their home talent could shine, and the outlaw steer was roped and tied. Not quickly, not easily, but it was work the cowboys knew. Tex McMullen was a prairie man.

He came out on Red Bird, a quick-kneed, nervous horse that fought his head and reared to go; but Tex reined him in nonchalantly, rolling his eyes at the line of mountain-boys as he watched for his steer to appear. There were curses from the corral, a clatter of horns and a cloud of dust; and then from the maelstrom the big steer rushed forth, head up and out for blood.

"Blaaa!" he bawled as he hooked at a stampeding horseman. Then he straightened out and crossed the line. The flagman struck down and made a break for the fence, all the cowboys reined away; and as McMullen on Red Bird went charging out after him Mace could see his horse break its stride. Tex had built a wide loop, to encircle the long, curved horns, but just as he closed in on the bellowing outlaw his horse shied and spoiled the throw.

A high exultant yell went up from the cowboys as they saw the champion fail, and the grandstands took up the cheer. He was whirling too big a loop on too short a rope—there was no slack left for the throw. McMullen lashed his horse across the rump with his rope and forced him closer in; but just as he leaned forward to make his throw the steer turned and hooked with all his strength. In an instant the long horn was against Red Bird's breast, it sunk deep and hurled him back. The next moment the blood-mad brute bore horse and rider down and leapt over them, bawling with rage.

Field judges and cowboys went galloping out, to rescue the overthrown champion; but while others stopped, Mace Bowman dashed on, building a loop in his long, manila rope. They had laughed at him for that and nicknamed him Long Rope, but when he fell in behind the outlaw and shot out his noose he had thirty feet of slack. The loop fell true, Brown Jug turned to the left and yanked the loping animal flat. But the old steer was on the warpath and bounded up, red-eyed, his tongue lolling out at each blat. He charged, but Brown Jug dodged him, swift and agile, obeying the reins; and Long Rope swooped around to the left. He came up past the steer, threw his slack behind its rump, and spurred Brown Jug straight ahead. There was a jerk, and a snap, and the steer changed ends. His head was twitched back, both his hind feet were caught up and he landed on his side with a thump.

"Yeee—pah!" whooped the cowboys; the grandstands rose and cheered; but Tex McMullen was wild with rage.

"What the hell do you mean, busting my steer?" he yelled as Long Rope rode up grinning.

"Your horse is out," answered Mace, "and you're barred from using two. That old horse-killer was dangerous."

"That's right!" assented Tutlow, the Arena Director. "Now come on, boys—get around this horse. He's bad hurt and bleeding—don't let the women see him." And all together they bore Red Bird out.

"Next roper!" shouted Tutlow, flagging the corral boss and starter.

"Mace Bowman, from Túcumcari!" bellowed the announcer.

Then as a wild steer came prancing out Mace took after him, swinging his loop. He rode closer, rising up in his stirrups, and once more the long noose shot out. Like a slim hand, still guided by the will of the man behind it, the loop spread, settling over the head. Bowman jerked it tight and stepped off on the run while Brown Jug, his ears pointed, started off at right angles, his body braced for the shock.

There was a neck-breaking yank and the steer, caught off his feet, was twitched through the air like a leaf. He landed with a bump, a stunning jar that left him limp, and Mace went down his rope on the run. The great steer was just rising when he grabbed its hind-leg and slammed it flat on its back. Then with his knee against the hock he forced the hind-foot forward, slapping his loop over the two front feet. He drew the three together, crossed the bones and made his tie, while the stands gave cheer after cheer. When he threw up his hands and the flag went down the timers caught it at twenty-four and three-fifths.

That ended the day, as far as Long Rope was concerned, for he had made the best time there was; but the mountain-boys went hog-wild. They wound up the festivities with a wild horse race that made the Hash-knife men look like dudes. Working in pairs and regardless of danger they roped the fiery mustangs and saddled them in front of the stands, then in a grand hurly-burly of bucking horses and battling men they flogged their wild mounts around the track. Fences were smashed and riders thrown. But the back-country had conquered at last, and they had to put on a show.

CHAPTER XIII
THE CHAMPEEN EVERYTHING

WHISKY was flowing like water over the Long Horn bar when Mace Bowman rode down-town from the wagon, but after a drink with the crowd he slipped out the back way and lost himself in the night. The battle was not won—there was another day to go—and he crawled under his tarp and went to sleep. But long before daylight he awoke with a jerk to the spatter of rain on his cheek. Clouds were racing past the moon, the wind was lashing the greasewood and the outlook for the contests was poor; but when he roused up in the morning the storm had blown away, though the flat was a sea of mud.

Mace threw back his tarp and stamped on his boots before he stepped out into the mire, but as the sun rose bright and clear the park dried up like magic and the cowboys prepared for the parade. At the Hash-knife wagon the gaudy showmen put on their brightest silks, until at last even Long Rope caught the fever and discarded his blue jumper for a shirt. He borrowed a razor and shaved, and combed out his curly hair; but as he was searching through his war-bag for an old silk handkerchief Little Eva came galloping by.

"Good morning!" she cried, smiling radiantly, and he chucked the greasy war-bag aside.

"Git a good one!" he grumbled querulously. "Dress up, boy—have some style!"

Little Eva had smiled—and a smile like that had caused a seven years' war in the days of Helen of Troy. Cities had fallen and heroes were slain, and still the fair Helen smiled on. But Mace didn't know about that—and of course, she was Little Joe's girl.

The infield was still wet when before the crowded stands the Calf Roping contest began. Little Joe built his loop and held Punkin behind the line. Then as he waited for his calf he glanced towards the box where Colonel Jones sat in state. She was there—she was watching. He smiled. The calf came out straight, for Joe had friends in the corral, and ran straight when it crossed the line. Then the flag went down, Punkin darted forth and Barfoot tied to it the first throw. He hit the ground on the run, flanked the calf and crossed its feet, took two dallies, a half-hitch and raised his hands. The time was twenty-three and two-fifths and the mountain-boys raised a yell.

Little Joe was not a world-beater, but he never missed a throw. He was sure, rain or shine, fast or slow. The rest tried to beat him, but there was a slick place on the field, and several of their horses went down. Then Tex McMullen rode out on Scrambled Eggs, the fastest roping-horse in the world, and Little Joe held his breath. Tex built him a careful loop in his thirty-foot rope, he hooked his prancing mount with the spurs; but the calf did not come out. Scrambled Eggs fought his head and went into a sulk, and the uproar in the calf corral increased; then a sick-looking yearling sidled out of the chutes and McMullen glanced back insolently.

"Is that the best you can do?" he asked; and the wranglers nodded grimly. They knew every calf in the pen.

The calf trotted straight till he came to the line, but as the flag went down and he heard the horse behind him he cringed and sidled off to the left. He knew what was coming—he was educated. Tex reined out to head him, to send him straight down the field; but as he charged in to make his throw the calf broke his stride and turned as swiftly to the right. Scrambled Eggs slipped and caught himself, straightened out and charged again; but the calf was running like the wind.

He had seen the sweep of the cruel rope and now he was on his way.

With a curse Tex McMullen warped his mount across the rump and took after him in a shower of clay. They ran and raced, ducked and dodged, turned back and started again, and still Tex withheld his throw. If he missed he was out for good. The seconds were ticking off but there was still time to win. He whirled, spurred in desperately, and threw. The loop encircled the head, but it slipped down before the jerk—under the belly, down the rump, off behind—and the writhing little calf leapt free.

"Ee-whoo!" whooped the grandstand, the cowboys, the chute-tenders; and Little Joe hugged Punkin and wept. He had won—the calf-roping was his!

McMullen galloped down the field, coiling his rope up as he cursed, building a loop that was small, very small. He leaned over and made his throw, popping the noose on inexorably. He yanked the calf flat and tied him in jig-time. But all the time he knew he had lost.

"You're a hell of a bunch!" he railed as he rode back to the corral where the grinning chute-tenders stood. "That dodrammed calf was educated!"

"I thought you liked 'em that way!" mocked a calf-wrangler, and McMullen whipped away in a rage. The year before he had made a clean sweep of the three main events of the Rodeo, but now he could see with half an eye that the cards were stacked against him. Already he had lost a thousand dollar prize when he had it almost in his hands, and as the Cowboy Bucking Contest began he was filled with grave forebodings. Sam Hockaday drew a bronk that was a man-eating fool, but he rode her and won a great hand. He had made a good ride the day before, and the judges were all local men. The only way for Tex to beat him was to make the ride of his life, and he stepped out with a smile.

"Te-ex McMullen!" bawled the big announcer, "on Little Elsie!" And the mountain-boys roared for joy. They had sawed off the LC mare on him.

They led her out then, a new horse and fighting her head, but Tex continued to smile. She was a bad one, of course, but the bronks were all bad and if he rode her he would win the purse.

"That's a nice, gentle horse," spoke up a voice at his elbow; and he turned to see Mace Bowman, also smiling.

"Why don't *you* ride one?" inquired McMullen, meaningly. "Ain't you the best cowboy in the world?"

"That's me!" drawled Mace, "but I ain't no hog. Saving up to win the steer-roping contest."

"Reckon you *could* ride her, though, if you wanted to?"

"Oh, sure—sure!" answered Long Rope, and laughed.

"Well! Hyer she is!" yelled a horse wrastler, impatiently; and McMullen turned back with a sigh. Something told him that Little Elsie was a wild, wild wolf that would paw the white out of the moon; and after riding her he would hardly be in shape for roping steers.

She fought her head and whirled, wiping the blinder off against her knee and cow-kicking whenever he approached; but Tex was a rider and he cinched her hard and fast before he hooked his toe in the stirrup. Then he swung up lightly and set himself in the saddle while he raised his quirt to strike.

"Turn her loose!" he said; and as her blinder was jerked back Tex struck.

Elsie cringed and crooked her neck, then she jumped straight up and McMullen gave a high whoop. She changed ends in the air, but he rode her like a bird and brought his quirt down again. The air was pierced by the shrill shrieks of women who sensed some imminent peril, every man in the park gave a yell. Then Elsie rose again, leaping higher than before, and the tall Texan set himself for the jar. But this time her stiff legs yielded. She sank down almost to the ground, and Tex's feet struck the earth with a bump. It was her old-time trick, which had busted Hockaday at the ranch, and McMullen lost one stirrup. She whirled like a cat as she felt his grip loosen, bawling and grunting, jumping up and landing hard. Then, quick as lightning, she turned the other way and the Champion of the World hit the grit.

For a moment there was silence as he lay in the dirt, but as he came alive the grandstands roared. The Champion had fallen—he had suffered defeat again! Little Elsie had taken down his pride. He rose up stiffly, wiping the mud out of his eyes, and suddenly the shouting ceased. Then as if out of space a resonant voice spoke forth:

"Pick that dirt out of yo' ear!" it mocked.

"Go to hell!" snarled McMullen, glowering at friend and foe alike, and the portentous voice spoke again.

"The Champeen Everything of the World! And busted by Little Elsie!"

Tex whirled like a flash and made for Mace Bowman, who was laughing as he faced the huge crowd. "Can you ride her?" he demanded, thickly.

"Oh, sure—sure!" responded Long Rope bluffly. "I ride that kind by day's works."

"You're a dodrammed liar!" yelled Tex in a frenzy, "They ain't a man here that can touch her!"

"What—Elsie?" repeated Mace, as the crowd paused to listen. "She's nothing but an old range mare!"

"You just brought her in here to bust me!" charged McMullen. "She's an outlaw! I say you can't ride her!"

"And I say," came back Bowman, suddenly flashing his roll, "I say, by grab, I can!"

"Aw—you and your phony money!" scoffed Tex; but he limped off, muttering to himself.

"Money talks!" observed Long Rope, oracularly; and tucked the roll back into his shaps.

Up in the stands James G. Cramer rose grandly, holding a big sheaf of greenbacks aloft.

"Even money," he offered, "that Bowman can ride Little Elsie. Any takers?" And he glanced towards

Colonel Jones. But the Colonel in his box was listening attentively to his wife, and Cramer bowed and sat down.

"Wo-orld's Cham-peen-ship Ste-eer Roping Contest!" the announcer bawled through his megaphone; and the Roman holiday went on. The first steer out the chutes went clear across the track and hit the back fence with a crash. The second one turned and fought the roper. But when Mace Bowman's name was called he rode out blithely and the grandstands gave him a cheer.

"Go after him, Túcumcari!" yelled the bleachers. "Bust him, Cowboy!"

"Whoopeelah!" returned Bowman, holding up his big noose; and the crowd came back with a roar. Then a huge mountain steer with moss on his horns ambled swiftly out of the pen and a solemn silence fell.

Mace shook out his loop, balanced so evenly for the throw, and touched Brown Jug with the spurs. Jug rose up on his hind legs and came down like a cat. The flag fell and he was off like the wind. Straight out across the field ran the steer, head up and with battle in his eyes; and behind him, running faster, came valiant Brown Jug while his master poised for the throw. He rose in the stirrups, a great coil in his left hand, and shot out the whirling loop. Far, far ahead it sped, encircling the wide horns, and Long Rope jerked it tight.

There was a yell from the crowd, cut short at its start, for the great steer had fallen flat. The next moment Brown Jug hit the same slippery streak, struggled gamely and went to the ground. Macc Bowman had hopped back to step off and make his tie when he hurtled like a bat through the air. He came down against the flank of the busted steer, which was just setting its hind-feet to get up. But at the first upward heave Mace grabbed the underleg and shoved it far to the front. He held it with one knee while from under his belt he whipped out an extra tie-string. Then, grinning in triumph, he looped the two front feet and drew all three of them tight. Two dallies, a half-hitch, and he threw up his hands, while the flag of the tie-judge snapped down.

There was a tumult in the timers' stand as the three watches were compared, a shout and rush of men.

"Twenty-one seconds!" reported the timers, and the announcer raised his megaphone.

"Ma-ace Bow-man!" he bellowed, "has beaten the Wo-orld's record! His time is twen-ty-one seconds! Previous record—twen-ty-two and three-fifths! By Tex Mc-Mullen of West-ern Shows!"

CHAPTER XIV THE CONQUEROR

GREAT renown had come to the El Toro Pioneer Day—a World's Record had been made in their park. The Western Shows champion had been shoved off the boards, defeated in three events by three men. The whole contest was called off while excited cowboys circled the track, bearing Mace Bowman on their shoulders. And behind them, no less honored, came Little Joe and Sam Hockaday—all conquerors of the Champion Everything!

There were protests, of course, and Colonel Jones from his box denounced the whole performance as a farce, but the timers were authorized men and their watches agreed. The twenty-one seconds would hold. To be sure, steer and horse and rider had gone down, but they had all passed over the line first. The throw had been made, the steer busted and tied. But it never could happen again!

Mace was riding round and round on the broad shoulders of old Ben Hockaday, struggling vainly to get to the ground, when Tex McMullen, lips curling, approached.

"That time is no good!" he yapped, fiercely. "The whole dam' business was framed!"

"All right," nodded Long Rope, serenely. "I'm the Champion of the World, all the same."

"You're the champeen cow-thief!" Tex came back savagely, but Bowman only laughed. He was standing in the midst of a group of admirers when McMullen came bounding back.

"Hey!" he called, "I'll go you on that bet. I dare you to ride Little Elsie!"

"Aw, you're jealous!" scoffed Mace. "Go off and soak your head. What are you trying to do—get me killed?"

"I'm trying to show you up for a cheap, small-town

sport. You jest broke that record by accident. But I'll bet my last dollar you cain't ride Little Elsie, and if you don't you're a dadburned coward!"

"Don't you do it! Don't you do it!" clamored the crowd. But Long Rope had fetched out his roll.

"All right, Mr. Man," he said. "We'll see who's the small-town sport. Now, how much money have you got?"

"Well—only eleven dollars!" confessed McMullen; and all but Bowman laughed.

"There you are," he said, counting out the money. "How much do you want on that hat?"

"I don't want to bet it," began Tex, but at the first laugh he saw he was stuck.

"Sixty dollars," he said at last.

"All right," agreed Mace. "That's a nice pair of spurs you've got. I wouldn't mind having that shirt. How about a hundred dollars against them and your shaps? That is, if you call yourself a sport!"

"Oh, I'll bet 'em!" gritted McMullen. "I know you cain't ride her. Only hope she breaks your danged neck."

"Put 'em up, then!" directed Bowman; and as Tex stripped off his shirt the big crowd burst into a laugh.

"Now!" announced Long Rope in the resonant carrying voice that made his every word plain, "I'm going to show you Main Street cowboys how a real hand rides a bronk. Bring out Little Elsie! Any one else want to bet?"

"Even money!" shouted Cramer, flashing his greenbacks again. "Even money that Bowman rides her!"

"I'll accept that wager!" replied Colonel Jones, rising up. "In any amount you name."

"Very well," nodded Cramer, walking over to him. "An even two thousand dollars."

"Well—er—that's quite a large sum," observed the Colonel, searching his pockets. "Would my personal check be acceptable?"

"Yes, indeed!" assented Cramer. "And if you'll accept mine as well I'll wager you five thousand more."

Jones made a wry face as he brought out his note book, but when Cramer examined the check there was no sign that the Colonel had heard.

"How about that five thousand?" he inquired, raising his eyebrows; but the autocrat waved him away.

"That is all," he said, and the barkeep smiled thinly. The Colonel's grandstand bluff had been called.

As Little Elsie came racking out, fighting her head and snorting loudly, the crowd settled down expectantly. Here at last was an event from which El Toro would date time, whether Túcumcari won or lost. If he rode Little Elsie after she had thrown Tex McMullen, the claims of that gentleman to the title of Champion Bronk Rider would go into complete eclipse. And if he lost—but Bowman had not lost.

"Ear her down!" he directed as four hardy horse-wrastlers halted Elsie in front of the stands; and while one snubbed the hackamore to the horn of his saddle another reached across for Elsie's ears. Then as he twisted them sharply to distract her attention Mace cinched his saddle on tight.

"Never mind the blind!" he said. "She's just a gentle old mare."

He stepped back, looking her over; and Little Elsie, her body twisted, stood watching, every muscle a-tremble. She was all set to begin her whirling series of back-jumps that would rattle a man all to pieces. That was her natural way of bucking and it had worked on Sam Hockaday and Tex McMullen, so Elsie would try it again. But Mace had been studying Little Elsie and he had figured another way out. If he could break up that whirling at the start he could ride her like a goat.

"Turn her loose!" he ordered, suddenly taking the reins and grabbing Little Elsie by one ear. Then he twisted the ear down, laying hold of her cheek-strap, and stuck his little finger into her eye. He could feel her eyelid tremble as she jerked back, half-blinded, and promptly swung up into the saddle. With his right hand he pulled her head straight, took his finger from her eye, and jabbed her in the belly with both spurs.

Little Elsie let loose everything, bucking straight up and straight ahead, mountainous waves of furious action that looked like sudden death but were nothing compared to that whirl.

In her excitement she had run the first jump, for those spurs were grollicking her vitals. No matter where she turned they impelled her straight ahead, and Mace was riding high. Snatching off his big hat he slapped her in the face, keeping her mind on anything else but that whirl. But at the end of the arena, when she fetched up against the fence, Little Elsie remembered her tricks.

Down went her head, she twisted her body like a snake, jumped high and came down—crouching. But Long Rope had seen her try that before and his feet did not strike the ground. He hooked her with both spurs, slamming her over the head with his hat, and Elsie came out of it, bawling. Straight up and down she jumped, wheezing and coughing as her breath came short, and the stands set up a cheer. She was weakening —she was ready to quit!

But Bowman was weakening, too. His iron knee-grip was slipping. He was dizzy, and his eyes saw red. Then, just as he looked around for a soft place to light on, Little Elsie settled down with a grunt. All the horse-wrastlers in the park came charging for the pick-up. One grabbed the hackamore, another reached for Mace and lifted him off as he passed.

"Whoopeelah! Túcumcari!" they shouted; and bore him back to the crowd.

CHAPTER XV THE LADY IN BLACK

THE Rodeo was over, as far as the mountain-men were concerned, when Long Rope rode Little Elsie. They swarmed down out of the stands, whooping and laughing and rushing to meet him and hoist him up on their shoulders. But when the uproar was at its height Colonel Jones rose majestically and made his way out of the park. All his box-party followed dutifully; but as Little Eva left she turned back and waved her hand at the conqueror.

He was riding high on Ben Hockaday's broad shoulders and in his arms, as symbols of victory, he bore Tex McMullen's shirt, his shaps and spurs and his big white hat. His curly hair was wind-tossed, his eyes big with laughter; and every time they stopped and called for a speech he responded with the same familiar words.

"Oh, that's nothing, boys. We ride bronks like that every day—over at Túcumcari!"

Then they brought Brown Jug and told him to mount, but he waited to put on Tex's shirt. Of all the gaudy shirts in the big parade there was none half so glorious as Tex's. Mace had spotted it the first day—a rich yellow, like cloth of gold, with *fleur-de-lis* in deepest purple—such a shirt as a king might wear. A purple neckerchief went with it, and on top of his old hat he set Tex's white beaver sombrero. Only showmen and rich cattlemen wore hats like that, as glossy and smooth as a beaver's belly—Seven X, the finest made.

They crushed through the doors of the Long Horn in a body, each intent on paying for the drinks; but when Mace raised his glass to drink to his great victory it tasted like cold tea.

"What's this?" he asked, eying Cramer suspiciously.

"Rye whisky—out of my own private bottle!" returned the barkeep suavely. "I'll tell you about it, later."

"What's the matter with right now?" demanded Long Rope. "Or is this an old ladies' tea?"

"It's on *account* of the ladies!" replied Cramer, with a wink. "You've got a lot of admirers, Mr. Bowman, and we want you to be at your best. And—ah—especially as, at the Cowboys' Ball tonight, you will meet the Lady In Black!"

"The which?" inquired Mace, leaning closer.

"Just a minute!" spoke up Cramer. "Boys, I know you'll excuse me! Something important to tell Mr. Bowman!"

He hustled Mace around through the milling crowd to the quiet of a card room behind and seated him with a smile.

"Here's your money," he said, patting his pocketbook. "You get half of that two thousand I won. But I'll keep it, if you don't object, because the Hash-knife men are sore. They're poor losers—always were. But as I was about to say, at our ball tonight you will meet the élite of El Toro. All our charming ladies will be present—you will fairly bask in their smiles—but there is one in particular whom we all delight to honor who will act as the Cowgirl Queen. And, to quiet the lying aspersions of your enemies that you broke the world's record while drunk, we want you to be perfectly sober. That is why I gave you cold tea for whisky—the only kind I drink, myself."

"O.K.," nodded Long Rope. "If that's the way you feel I'll take another snifter of cold tea. But who is this Lady In Black that you mentioned out at the bar?"

Cramer pressed the button and as the drinks were served he got around to answer the question.

"She is a charming little lady who, to tell the truth, is really quite taken with you. But on account of parental disapproval she will not be able to attend the Ball. Or that is, not till midnight. But promptly at twelve o'clock, wearing black and masked with a black domino, she will appear and crown you King of the Cowboys!"

"Who—me?" exclaimed Mace, rising up. "I'm going on a drunk."

"Oh, no!" smiled Cramer, "if you knew the lady, I'm sure you would never consider it! And another thing, Brother Bowman, have you forgotten the fact that you must soon stand trial for cow-theft? That is a very serious charge in this part of the country, where so much wholesale rustling is going on, and your friends have combined to protect you against yourself. We don't want you to go to the Pen."

"And I don't want to go!" answered Long Rope, earnestly. "So I'll take the pledge, right now."

"Very well," agreed the barkeep. "You're a brainy man, Bowman. I believe we can get you clear. Now go down to Phat's Barber Shop and get a bath and a clean shave. Neil Monroe will fit you out with clothes. But the Queen has especially requested that you wear McMullen's shirt—the one you won in the contest."

"The Queen, eh?" repeated Mace. "Is she the same girl as this Mysterious Lady In Black?"

"The same—and the most charming little creature in the world!"

"Well, well!" observed Bowman, "this is certainly mysterious. But at the same time, Brother Cramer, I can see you're my friend. And I don't want to go to the Pen."

"There you are!" nodded the barkeep, approvingly. "There's where your native intelligence comes out. We are all here to help you, and since I find you so receptive just cast your eye over this."

He drew a printed dodger from his pocket and spread it out on the table.

"Our announcement for the Ball," he stated. "I'll explain why your name is there, later."

COW-THIEVES' BALL!
AT THE SCHOOLHOUSE * * * * * TONIGHT!

COMMITTEE ON QUALIFICATIONS.

Satchel Vest Steen	Joe Barfoot
Tex McMullen	Mace Bowman
Sowbelly Johnson	Phat Noland

THIS IS A GOOD LIVE COMMITTEE. THEY KNOW THEIR STUFF.

If you fail to qualify before this Committee, you may appeal to Col. Breckenridge Jones of the Cattle Sanitary Board, whose decision is final. If you can't get by with him it's your own fault. You can't dance, so keep off the floor!

THE MYSTERIOUS LADY IN BLACK WILL APPEAR AT MIDNIGHT!
COME ONE! COME ALL!
NO COW-THIEVES BARRED!

"Well, by grab!" gasped Mace. "That's plain enough!"

"Yes, yes! But let me explain! This is really our regular Cowboys' Ball. But the idea is to make the Hash-knife outfit mad, so none of them will attend. If they do, you see, they admit that they are cow-thieves, duly qualified by Colonel Jones."

"Yes, but what about *my* name being down here for a cow-thief? I never stole that calf!"

"Why, certainly not!" smiled Cramer. "That's where the joke comes in! And to show there's no hard feelings, Phat Noland has consented to lend his name! But everybody in the county knows that the Hash-knives are branding mavericks! And Breckenridge Jones is on the Sanitary Board, that is supposed to stop all that. It will do you a lot of good when it comes to the trial, calling attention as it does to the undoubted fact that Jones is stealing, himself. But the biggest kick of all is —not a Hash-knife man will be there! We'll have the dance all to ourselves!"

"Well—all right!" agreed Bowman. "If you're sure it's a joke!"

"It's the joke of the century—a horse on Colonel Jones! Our friends will laugh their heads off!"

"Let her go, then," shrugged Long Rope. "But the first man that calls me a cow-thief—"

"No, no! You don't understand!" laughed Cramer. "We *all* call each other cow-thieves! It's just like the ear-sign among the NAI. It's a cow-sign, but that don't make us cows!"

"Keno!" beamed Mace. "I'm on. Now lead me to this cow-thief, Phat Noland!"

"That's the boy!" praised the barkeep. "I knew you'd understand." And he pushed him out the side door.

Phat Noland's shop had every chair taken, but when Bowman came in the Roughriding Barber dropped everything.

"Hello, you old cow-thief!" he shouted genially. "Come to get that bath and shave? Well, step right in and we won't keep you waiting, for we know how valuable your time is. And another thing, Brother Bowman, the merchants of this town know you ain't no tightwad, like McMullen. So, to show our appreciation, this bath and shave is free—also a shine and shampoo."

He unlocked the bathroom door, where the tub of hot water was waiting, and ran a string around Long Rope's waist.

"Just taking your measure," he explained, "for that pair of pants, from Monroe. I'll send my boy down, and before you're ready to dress Neil will send the pants up—free. They ain't nothing too good for a roper like you, Mace. El Toro is sure proud of that record. And when it comes to bronks, you're the riding fool of the world. I remember when I was in

Tucson and made that record as the Champion Roughriding Barber of the World—but all right, I'll tell you about it later."

He ducked out of the bathroom and, just as Bowman was ready to dress, passed a package through the door.

"Suit of underwear there, too," he called. "And some nice silk socks. But don't forget—you want to wear Tex's shirt!"

A half an hour later when Mace stepped out, he was the last word in frontier elegance. His new gray pants were stuffed into his boots, which had been polished from top to toe; and, tucked into the pants, was the golden shirt with *fleur-de-lis* which McMullen had unwillingly contributed. The Roughriding Barber made much of him while he shampooed him and slicked down his curls, not forgetting to relate all the details of his own record-breaking exploit. It seemed the cowboy that he shaved had been drunk, and the horse had pitched every jump; but though he had only cut him once some of his friends had had the nerve to blame Phat.

The Bon Ton Restaurant gave an impromptu free supper to Mace and a group of chance friends, and then as the time for the dance approached they adjourned to the El Toro Schoolhouse. Already the benches had been set along the walls, the musicians were ready to go; but before the Grand March the Committee begged the privilege of presenting Mr. Bowman to the ladies.

It was all very flattering to a man charged with

grand larceny, and within a week of his trial, and Long Rope made the most of it. He laughed and shook hands and asked the favor of a dance, until at last the fiddles struck up. Then in a mad whirl of revelry the time passed so swiftly that midnight came on them unaware.

A closed carriage rolled up and halted outside the door. Startled messengers rushed to and fro. Then James G. Cramer as master of ceremonies turned the lights down for the entry of the Queen. She was tall and willowy, dressed in a long black gown trimmed with filmy Spanish lace. A high tortoiseshell comb supported her mantilla, through the flowered veil of which a white face could be glimpsed, half-masked by a dainty domino. It was the Mysterious Lady In Black!

She halted in the doorway, standing regally aloof as she gazed about the room; then with quick, graceful steps she went straight to Mace Bowman and laid her hand on his arm.

"I have come," she announced, in a deep, throaty contralto, "to crown you King of the Cowboys! But first we will have a waltz!"

She nodded to the orchestra, which struck up *Sobra Las Olas,* and before he knew it Mace was floating across the room with the Mysterious Lady in his arms. She was so buoyant, so slender, that she seemed almost a wraith; and her high-heeled slippers as she glided away were too small for earthly feet. They were more like the shoon of some dainty fairy queen than thosc of a Lady In Black. But her steps were swift and spritely, and the hand that clutched his own was warm and pulsating with life.

"What a wonderful shirt you are wearing, Your Majesty!" she observed as they whirled down the hall. "Did you choose the colors yourself?"

Long Rope leaned a little closer to see if she was laughing, but she turned her face away.

"No, Queen," he answered. "But I'm sure glad you like it. I won this riding that bronk!"

"Yes, I saw you," she breathed, leaning closer in turn but with her eyes cast modestly down. "Every moment I thought you would fall. And oh, how my heart beat! I am proud to crown you King! Will you remember me, when I am gone?"

"Never could forget you!" he answered fervently. "You sure are the Queen of the World! And say, you know how to dance!"

"I could dance on with you forever!" she sighed. "But my carriage is waiting! I must go!"

"Just one more whirl!" he pleaded as the orchestra came to a stop. "Start her up, boys!" And he nodded to the leader. Then, willy-nilly, he took her across the floor and they waltzed on as in a dream. Not a word was spoken, she avoided his gaze, and all too soon the haunting music ceased and imperiously she set herself free. James G. Cramer stepped up and handed her Long Rope's hat—the creamy-white beaver he had won—and she raised it above his head.

"I crown you," she pronounced, "King of Cowboys! And Champion Everything!"

Then with a laugh she rammed it down over his curly locks and darted for the door. But something about that laugh aroused a sudden suspicion. Her queenly voice had been a deep contralto, but this was a high soprano. There was an impish note of mischief about it that went well with "Champion Everything," and he caught up with her as she reached the door.

"Make way, boys!" he commanded, putting his arm about her waist and whisking her through the crowd; and at the door of the carriage, as she leapt lightly in, the black mask fell away. For an instant she looked up at him from the protecting gloom and he saw that her eyes were blue. Blue and wistful and full of laughter! Then she slammed the door and was gone.

As the carriage whirled away Bowman stood amazed, unmindful of all the world. This tall Lady In Black with the deep contralto voice, had the eyes of Little Eva!

He was roused by a harsh voice, close at hand in the darkness, and McMullen loomed above him menacingly.

"So you're trying to steal my girl, hey?" he said. "Well, have a good time, King. We'll soon have you in the stray-pen, wearing a shirt with a broad stripe down the back. Don't forget that Hash-knife calf!"

CHAPTER XVI "HERE GOES NOTHING!"

UNTIL almost day, Long Rope danced on with the fair daughters of El Toro, but he could not forget the Queen. Nor could he forget that harsh warning of Tex McMullen's—about the stray-pen and the shirts with broad stripes. The night had been full of both bitter and sweet, and his head was in a whirl. For though he held other maidens in his arms his thoughts were all of Little Eva. She had braved the anger of her father to be present and crown him King, and her first words had been veiled in mystery. But at the end, when she let slip the domino, she had revealed her real, laughing self.

He could have sworn that, through the veil, her eyes had been dark, her hair black, her accent Spanish; and it was to her that his soul had gone out. She was so tall, so stately, so vibrant with emotion, so deep-voiced and every inch a queen! And then at the end, despite her mask and high comb, she was suddenly Little Eva, Joe's girl!

But as he stood there in the dark gazing after her, another and more sinister voice had shattered his new-born dreams. The Hash-knives were on his trail, they were out to get him, and Tex McMullen would swear to anything. It would take all the power of the NAI to keep him from going to the Pen.

Mace woke up late, and his dreams had been uneasy

—dreams where good and evil were inextricably mingled, and grief and happiness hopelessly mixed. But the sun was in the sky, he was well and strong and free—and the Champion Steer Roper of the World! There was money in Cramer's safe to retain a good lawyer, and every man in town was his friend—the Hash-knife gang had gone home.

There were some hold-over drunks in the Long Horn Saloon—men who argued unceasingly or wept or shook hands—and Mace was glad he was not one of them. No more whisky for him—he had had his warning from the one man who ought to know best. James G. Cramer drank nothing but tea. But as if to refute his arguments Red Tutlow came pattering in, as happy as a lark, and he drank a full quart every day.

"How's the Champeen Everything?" he greeted as he leaned one elbow on the bar. "Come up and have one with me. Say, Cramer and I want to have a talk with you. About this trial, next week."

He tossed off his whisky without raising an eyebrow and led the way into the regions behind. Here in the private card rooms, cut off from interruptions and noise, half the business of El Toro was transacted. Cattle were bought and sold, oil options and leases dosed, and in one of them James G. Cramer took his ease. Before him on the table lay high piles of greenbacks, the proceeds of three long, festive days; but he chucked them all away after a swift check and pressed the button for the drinks.

"Well, Mace, my boy," he said, you made a very

good impression. And especially with the ladies. But a jury is composed of men. It's time we got down to business about this matter of the Hash-knife calf."

"I've got an idea, boys!" beamed Red, "and a good one! Let Cramer plead this case! A lawyer can't do anything, for the simple reason that there's no denying the facts. Joe killed the calf and Mace had a beefsteak, and they've got three witnesses to prove it. But for this solemn line of bunk—about Mace's sore eye and Little Joe's concern for his friend—there's no one can handle it like James!"

"Ah, thank you, Red!" bowed Cramer and glanced expectantly at Mace.

"We-ell," said Bowman, at last, "I reckon you're right. But we don't want to make any mistake. I woke up this morning in a sweat, dreaming that shirt of mine had big, black stripes."

"No, but here's the point," went on Tutlow, "Cramer has got this all planned out. He knows every move to hornswoggle that jury and make them forget the facts. But if you hire a lawyer, with his yammering and objections and making everybody sore, the jury will settle down to the law and the evidence—and right there you and Joe will lose."

"I reckon so," assented Mace with a sigh.

"Go ahead!" nodded Red to Cramer, "and tell him about the District Attorney."

"Our District Attorney," began Cramer, "is up for reelection next fall. And while of course he points with pride to his record of convictions, that doesn't always bring in the votes. Here we have two young men, both personally popular and having a host of friends, accused by the Hash-knife company of grand larceny of a calf. I have talked with Mr. Clemens on the vote-getting aspects of this case, and while he will have to rave and rant and denounce the stealing of cattle, it is tacitly understood that he is in favor of improving North America. By that I mean the complete elimination of Colonel Jones from our midst.

"Now to make the case stick it is necessary, of course, that Clemens should denounce all cow-thieves, and you and Joe in particular. But that is just his professional gesture and you boys must not take offense. Then he will call in his three witnesses, to prove that the calf was killed, and produce the hide—Exhibit A—and all that. This is something we can't disprove, so the defense won't say a word.

"In a case like this, boys, with the evidence all against us, we've got to laugh it out of court; and this District Attorney is a solemn ass who likes to play the clown. And, playing right into our hand, the Judge is an Eastern man. I've had the pleasure of meeting Judge Henshaw, and over the glasses he confessed that the West had intrigued him greatly. He is out for local color and bull-con stories to tell at the club when he gets home. So let's give him a steer—a Texas steer—and he'll let us play horse with the law.

"When it comes to the trial I want you, Mace, to get up and tell the Judge something like this. On account of the enormous wealth and influence of Colonel

Jones—as an oil magnate and member of the Sanitary Board—there isn't a lawyer in the County that you can depend on to stand up against him. So, being confident of your innocence and the open-mindedness of the jury, you will request that your case be presented by your loyal friend, James G. Cramer.

"That's your privilege, according to law, and the District Attorney has already agreed not to object. Then the fireworks will begin and we'll let Clemens have the best of it. Let him orate and paw the ground and shake his long finger and build up an air-proof case. After that I'll call on Joe Barfoot to tell about your licking Gilhooly. That will bring up the matter of your eye. Joe will tell how you were suffering from the terrible blow of this slugger in the Colonel's employ, and how as an act of mercy he was moved to get you a steak.

"That's our story, and we're going to stick to it. You were brutally used by this hired bouncer, who makes a business of beating up cowboys, and if we can ring in that story about Meals Twenty-five Cents it will get a big laugh out of the jury—who, needless to say, will be cowmen. This will show Colonel Jones in a very bad light, as a man lacking in the common impulses of humanity; and then I'll call on you, Mace.

"Now we all know, of course, that you're bright as a dollar; but for the purposes of our story you'll act the part of a fool. All you'll say is 'Yes' and 'No,' and I'll turn you over to the District Attorney. He'll fly right into you, to prove you a liar, but you answer 'I don't know' to everything. Just state that your mind is a blank on the events of that particular day, on account of the heavy blows of Gilhooly, Jones's agent, who was hired to beat you up. I hope that isn't asking too much?"

"Oh, no!" responded Bowman. "Go ahead."

"Well," went on Cramer, mysteriously, "the District Attorney will ask you a certain question, to which I alone have the answer. And that answer, my boy, will bring down the house and send you forth a free man."

"Yes, but what is the answer?" demanded Mace.

"It can be sprung only once," responded Cramer, gravely. "I'll tell you on the morning of the trial."

"Well, what's the question, then?"

"The District Attorney," explained Cramer, "is going to express doubts about your mind being a blank. And to prove that you are faking he'll try to find out what you know. When he asks you if you know what a maverick is—hold your breath, boys—the big blow-off will take place."

"And have I got to take a chance on that one smart answer to keep me out of the Pen?"

"You have!" replied the barkeep. "Unless, of course, you prefer the law."

"Nope! He hasn't got a look-in," spoke up Red; and Long Rope drew a deep breath.

"Well, here goes nothing!" he said at last. "I'll go you, if I lose!"

CHAPTER XVII
DEFINITION OF A MAVERICK

MACE Bowman was in a sweat when he emerged from Cramer's office and considered on what a hair his fate was hung. One funny answer to a question—and how did he know it was funny? According to Cramer, this single response would be sufficient to convulse the court and turn him and Little Joe free. It would reverse the testimony of three competent witnesses that he and Joe had killed the calf. The law and the evidence would be forgotten. And all on account of some wisecrack about: What is an *orejano* or maverick?

Mace was still in a sweat when, a few days later, he was led, in the custody of Mordecai Byrnes, to have his day in court. There was something about the cold and jaundiced eye of the sheriff that reminded him of bars and jails, and even the smiling assurance of James G. Cramer failed to lift the great weight off his mind. He had all the sensations of a man doing lock step in the company of desperate felons, and yet his heart told him he was perfectly innocent of even the intent to do wrong.

All he remembered was that his eye had been hurting him and Little Joe had mentioned a steak. Or maybe *he* had mentioned it. And then Joe had gone out and killed an *orejano* and put the beef over his eye.

Well, men had gone to prison for less than that, and especially if it was Company beef. It made no difference if the ears were slick—the calf had carried the Hash-knife brand. Mace glanced about hopelessly as he entered the crowded room—for all El Toro was there to behold—and right up in front he saw Breckenridge Jones, Mort Steen and Tex McMullen!

Colonel Jones sat up so straight he leaned over backward, Satchel Vest had his lips pouted purposefully; and Tex McMullen, as he regarded his enemy, gave way to a cynical smile. Here were three of a kind, and a hard hand to beat if Mace was any judge; and beside them, staring out through windowpane glasses, was the District Attorney, Clemens. He was tall and horse-faced and deferential to a degree to the Colonel, who was the complaining witness; but there was something about the mock solemnity of his countenance that gave a ray of hope.

There was a lot of formality about reading the charges and selecting a jury, all cattlemen; and then Clemens opened the case.

"Your Honor and gentlemen of the jury," he began, "in the case of the People *versus* Joe Barfoot and Mace Bowman, we shall prove that, on or about the fifth day of May, they did willfully, feloniously, and unlawfully kill a calf, said calf being the property of Breckenridge Jones."

He then went on to state the facts regarding their arrest and examination and called Colonel Jones to the stand.

"Calling your attention to the fifth day of May, of the present year, where were you, Colonel Jones?"

"I was at my ranch, at Bottomless Spring!" responded the Colonel, stiffly.

"And did you, at that time, encounter the defendants in this case? And if so, please relate the circumstances."

"Yes, I encountered them both!" replied Jones, his black eyes gleaming balefully. "In the act of butchering one of my calves!"

Bowman sank down deeper in his chair as the Colonel related the circumstances; and after Steen and McMullen had corroborated his testimony the whole world seemed to turn black. But all the time in his place beside them James G. Cramer, the special pleader for the defense, retained his calm and unruffled smile. They had proved three times over that his clients were guilty, but locked behind his lips he held the Open Sesame which would free them from the doors of prison.

What those magic words were had not been revealed, but as Pelion was piled upon Ossa with fresh evidence of their guilt he smiled and bided his time. With a negligent wave of the hand he declined to cross-examine the witnesses, he turned a deaf ear to the reading of the law; and when at last the District Attorney closed his argument he put Little Joe on the stand.

"Your Honor and gentlemen of the jury," he began, "I know nothing of the law. All I know is that my friends here are innocent of any intent to commit a crime. So if, in pleading their case, I should make any mistake I trust that Your Honor will correct me—or my learned opponent. Mr. Clemens. Not knowing the forms of legal procedure I can do no more than ask them to tell their own story, and let the jury be the judges of their guilt.

"I am not here, gentlemen, to seek to justify in any way the crime of stealing cattle. Although the value of a calf is in itself very small, the law has wisely designated the stealing of one a felony, and the punishment a term in State's Prison. But to constitute a crime the intent must be proven, and in this case my clients are guiltless. You all know them, my friends, as two rough and ready cowboys, not without renown as ropers and riders—good boys, but always ready for a frolic.

"It is my purpose, gentlemen of the jury, to prove, and beyond the peradventure of a doubt, that their motives in this case were meritorious. If I thought for a moment that Little Joe Barfoot had killed this calf for beef I should not be here to defend him. You all know Joe, and you knew his father before him—a man loyal and true to his friends. Mr. Barfoot, kindly tell the court your reasons for killing this calf."

"Well, you see," began Joe, "Mace had got in a fight and he had a terrible black eye. The blacksmith at Bottomless Spring had almost put it out, and when we left he could hardly see. So I says:

" 'What you need for that eye is a steak!' And I took after the first maverick I saw. It was a slick-ear and I shot it and cut out a chunk of beef, and put it over his eye. Well, that's all, but while he was laying down I went back to butcher the calf. It didn't seem right to let the meat go to waste. But when I went to skin it I found that some jasper had branded that calf on the sly. It was sleepered into the Hash-knife brand."

"Ah, excuse me," broke in Cramer, smiling. "Just what do you mean by that?"

"Well, some crazy cowboy had left the ears slick, and branded it on the hip. Then some time this fall, if nobody caught on, he'd earmark it and make a clean steal."

"You mean to intimate, Mr. Barfoot, that some Hash-knife employee was attempting to steal this calf?"

"I don't intimate nothing!" returned Little Joe, hotly. "They're doing it, all the time!"

"I object, Your Honor!" spoke up Clemens, smiling tolerantly. "We are dealing in this case with the theft of but one calf, with which the defendants are jointly charged. This testimony, therefore, is irrelevant, incompetent and immaterial and I ask that it be stricken from the records."

"Your Honor," protested Cramer, "I know nothing of such points, but if it is the custom of the plaintiff, or men in his employ, to illegally brand and steal calves, I consider that very relevant. It is a maxim of the law, I am told, that a man must come into court with clean hands ——"

"Objection overruled," said the Judge. "Proceed with your case, Mr. Cramer."

"I thank you," responded Cramer, bowing; and Bowman looked the Judge over curiously. He was a small, dapper man, with wise, violet-blue eyes that twinkled with hidden mirth. And, despite his judicial severity, it was evident he could see a joke.

"Well, the point is," went on Cramer, "that this calf in question had been previously and surreptitiously branded. I should like to ask, Mr. Barfoot, who would have benefited by this act, if the calf had not been killed."

"Why—him!" blared out Joe, pointing his finger at Colonel Jones. "Ain't he the owner of the brand?"

"I object!" shouted Clemens, and after another debate Cramer returned to the story of the steak.

"You were speaking, Mr. Barfoot, of a fight, in which your companion suffered an injury to his eyes. Kindly tell the gentlemen of the jury the circumstances that brought this on."

"Well, you all know, I guess," began Joe, "about this blacksmith at Bottomless Spring. He's a bouncer in the summertime with Western Shows and he whips every man that comes near. It's got so a cowboy don't hardly dare to git a drink, on account of this Martin Gilhooly. He's as big as a mountain and got a face on him like a baboon, and he's run all us boys away. But Bowman had had trouble at the Hash-knife wagon, on account of their trying to charge him for a meal—"

"Just a moment," interrupted Cramer. "Please tell the nature of this trouble."

"Well, Mace came riding in to the wagon, about

eight miles east of the spring, and the cook wanted to charge him for his meal. But Bowman stood him off and kept on eating—then he offered him a thousand dollar bill. Some prize money he'd won, over at Dallas. The cook couldn't change it and while they were quarreling Mr. Steen, the wagon-boss, rode up. They had some words then, about charging for meals in a country where lots of men had perished, and Mace and me rode away. He was mad, and his horse was thirsty, so we took a chance and went to the spring. Then when this big blacksmith began to order him around and dare him to git down and fight, Mace made him a bet of ten dollars against his anvil that he could lick him and throw him into the spring."

"Yes, yes! And what then?" inquired Cramer. And the Judge wiped away a smile.

"They had a big fight," grinned Barfoot, "and knocked the whole blacksmith shop down before Gilhooly hollered, 'Enough!' But he had to give in and then Mace grabbed the anvil and throwed it down the Bottomless Spring!"

"Order in the court!" bellowed the bailiff as the audience burst into a guffaw; and the Colonel looked distinctly annoyed.

"I-I—see!" nodded Cramer, smiling gravely. "And in this fight your friend got a black eye!"

"He got a terrible eye!" shrilled Little Joe. "So bad he could hardly see! Thc blacksmith slugged him, and then the roof fell down on him—he was bruised from his head to his heels. But Colonel Jones was mad because his bouncer had got licked, and just after I put this steak on Mace's eye, he and Steen and McMullen rode up. They were following along behind us to make trouble; and so—well, we was arrested."

"Very good," nodded Cramer. "That is all, Mr. Barfoot. You may take the witness, Mr. Clemens."

The District Attorney rose up slowly and pointed a long, lank forefinger at Joe. But as he propounded question after question Cramer leaned over and whispered in Bowman's ear. It was the magic answer which was to win their case, hands down—and when Long Rope heard it, he grinned.

"Don't forget, now!" warned Cramer. "And wait for the question. And remember—your mind was a blank!"

"Leave it to me!" answered Mace, laughing silently; and Clemens came to an end.

"And now," began Cramer, "I'll call Mr. Bowman to testify in his own defense. You all know him, gentlemen of the jury—the Champion Steer Roper of the World!"

"I-I—object!" thundered the District Attorney. "Irrelevant—incompetent—immaterial!"

"Objection sustained!" ruled the little Judge promptly; but he gazed at Mace with friendly eyes.

"Mr. Bowman," went on Cramer, "as I understand it, this calf was not killed for beef, but to get a steak for your eye."

"Yes, sir," responded Mace.

"Well, please tell the jury the circumstances which led up to this overt act?"

"Huh?" inquired Long Rope, gaping.

"I say, please tell the jury how you happened to get your eye hurt. And how you came to kill the calf."

"Well, I got in a fight with the blacksmith and he hit me awful hard, in the eye. Then he got me down and rubbed his beard in it, until I couldn't hardly see. We rode off then and I said to Joe—or maybe Joe said to me: 'What we need for that eye is a steak.' "

"Yes, yes," nodded Cramer. "Go on!"

"Well, I laid down under a tree and that's all I know, except that Joe came and brought me a steak."

"You have no recollection, then, of his killing the calf? Or of any of the succeeding events?"

"No, sir. My eye was hurting awful bad."

"That's all you know, then—that your eye was hurting you? As for the rest, your mind was a blank?"

"Yes, sir. That's all I know."

"You had no intent, then, of killing this calf? No knowledge of what was taking place? Your mind was a perfect blank."

"Yes, sir," responded Mace.

"Your Honor and gentlemen of the jury," began Cramer, "you have heard what my client has said. He was so cruelly beaten by this hired bruiser that his mind became a blank. He had lost all his power to think and act, and got down off his horse in a daze. I think this fact alone is sufficient ground for acquittal. He was out of his mind, his volition had fled; he has no knowledge even, of the act. I therefore ask the jury to return a verdict of 'Not guilty' in his case. That is all. You can take the witness."

He nodded to Clemens, the District Attorney, who arose with an exaggerated sneer.

"Your Honor," he said, "and gentlemen of the jury, I hardly thought that the special pleader for the defense would descend to this ancient device. If the mind of the defendant—and mind you, I say *if*—if his mind was a blank, how was he able to remember that his companion brought him a steak? It is all right to state that his mind was affected, but now let's get down to the facts. Mr. Bowman, what horse were you riding?"

"I don't know!" Mace answered, firmly.

"You don't remember, eh? Your mind was a blank, hey? Well, how many horses did you have? Did you have more than one?"

"I don't know!" responded Bowman, shaking his head.

"Isn't it a fact that you had but one horse, an animal called Brown Jug? And that you must have been riding on him?"

"I don't know. I suppose I was."

The District Attorney reared back and gazed at him contemptuously.

"Well, what do you know?" he asked. "Do you know what a maverick is?"

Mace raised his head and glanced from the Judge to the jury and back at James G. Cramer, who smiled and nodded encouragingly.

"W'y, yes," he said. "I do."

"Oh, you do, eh?" sneered Clemens. "Well, that's

good, that's fine. Now please tell the gentlemen of the jury, just what you think a maverick is."

"You mean an *orejano?*" inquired Mace.

"Yes—a maverick or *orejano!* Unless, of course, your mind is still a blank!"

"Oh, no!" responded Long Rope. "My mind is all right, now. A maverick is a little calf whose mother has died, and whose father has gone off with another cow!"

It was the magic answer which Cramer had whispered and the jury sat paralyzed in their seats. Then they threw back their heads and laughed and the Judge set his lips in a line.

"Order in the court!" shouted the bailiff, striking the table; but the magic had its way. He too burst out laughing, and all the court with him; and last of all the District Attorney.

"That's all!" he announced, sitting down.

"That's all!" nodded Cramer; and the Judge gave the case to the jury.

"Not Guilty!" they answered, without leaving their seats. And Mace and Little Joe went free.

CHAPTER XVIII
A HORSE ON THE COLONEL

IT was a great vindication of the jury's sense of humor, this acquittal of Mace and Joe, and a horse on Breckenridge Jones. He had come into court fully expecting a verdict of "Guilty" which would rid him of two troublesome interlopers; but an ordinary bar-keeper had outwitted the District Attorney, and even the Judge had laughed. The Colonel rose up arrogantly and with his eyes straight ahead, marched out of the courtroom in a pet.

But everybody else, except a few who rushed out to peddle the joke through the town, surged up to shake hands with Long Rope. It was a new one and a good one and, despite his protestations, Mace found himself set down as a wit. The foreman of the jury said it would be a crime to send a kidder like him to the Pen, and even suggested that he sue the Colonel for damages—for defamation of character!

"I'll do it, by grab!" declared Long Rope, laughing. And the rest of the jury stood in.

"You'll win!" they said. "Soak him good and plenty! Just ask for a jury trial! The people of this country are your *friends!*"

Mace could see that with half an eye, and Cramer stood by beaming as he saw what his joke had done. "Meet me down at the Long Horn," he whispered purposefully. "The Colonel shall pay for this insolence."

"Which insolence?" inquired Mace.

"Why, saying that you and Joe were cow-thieves! A man's good name is *property!*"

"All right," agreed Bowman, lightly. "We'll sue him for a million dollars! That is, if you'll plead the case! And all the money we win I'll spend over the Long Horn bar!"

"Now there's an idea," pronounced Cramer, "that should be given the most careful consideration! It contains great possibilities for the improvement of North America and the confusion of our enemy, Colonel Jones. Come down to the saloon, right away!"

He darted away as if impelled by some great thought, born Minerva-like from his brain; but Mace and Little Joe lingered on, to shake hands with numerous admirers. What a magic spell the artful Cramer had cast by his simple definition of a maverick! Even the Judge came down, after laying aside his robes, and congratulated them upon the unique defense. But as they stepped out of the courthouse door and strolled away together, hardly believing that once more they were free, Little Eva came running across the lawn and shook hands with them both at once.

"Oh, I'm *so* glad!" she exclaimed, gazing from one to the other. "And I heard about that poor little maverick! But I've got to skip or Daddy will see me. Come out and see me—both of you!"

"Heh!" laughed Long Rope, "I'd have to have a steak off an elephant to put on the next eye I'd get."

"Aw, never mind a little thing like that!" she mocked. "We'll kill the fatted calf."

Then she danced away among the broad, shady cottonwoods and they could see she was laughing yet.

"Old Cramer sure pulled a good one," observed Mace, "when he told me that gag about the calf. But who would think, Joe, that the Colonel's own daughter would come around to be in on the laugh!"

"She wants us to come and see her," said Barfoot in a transport. "Ain't she the prettiest little girl you ever saw?"

"Sure is," agreed Bowman. "But I know when I'm lucky and I'm staying away from that ranch."

"We can go some time when the Colonel is away and the boys are out on the circle."

"Well, you can," nodded Long Rope. "But excuse *me,* Mr. Barfoot. We dam' near went to the Pen. I got a lot of letters, and telegrams and everything, from California and Cheyenne and Pendleton, all asking me to come and take part in their Rodeos—and, boy, I'm going to do it. I'm the Champion Steer Roper of the World and I'm out to make some dough. But you're just as good—you beat Tex in the Calf Roping. Come along—let's get in on the prize money."

"Sure thing!" responded Joe. "We'll make the whole circle and show 'em we're no false alarms. All I hope is we strike some contest where Tex is going to compete—I hate that ornery whelp!"

"We'll make him look like a fool," predicted Bowman confidently. "But I sure wish I had that horse, Scrambled Eggs. You bet—he's quick as a flash. He's got us both beat for speed."

"Yes, but not for being steady! Old Punkin will skin him any time when it comes to slippery grounds and bad steers. Tex may win some of the day-money, but in a three-calf contest I'll clean him, every time!"

"Well, I sure cleaned him *once!*" chuckled Mace,

"and I've got his hat and spurs to prove it. And this here fancy shirt! Say, won't it make him look sick when I wear it up at Pendleton!"

"He's bad medicine, that hombre," grumbled Barfoot. "It ain't *his* fault we ain't in the Pen."

"No, and here's another tip," confided Long Rope. "He's claiming Little Eva for his girl."

"But she jest hates him!" cried Joe. "I can tell by her eyes! She hates the ground he walks on. The hell of it is, though, he's there with the show and can see her every day. They'll be off on the road now in a couple of weeks—"

"Well, let 'em go!" broke in Bowman, impatiently. "What do you want of a girl with a father like that? Or any girl? All you've got is a ranch and a little bunch of cows, and you never look after either one. Come on—be a man, and forget Little Eva. You haven't got a Chinaman's chance!"

"Didn't she jest come and shake hands with me—and ask me to come and see her? I believe, by grab, you're jealous! But you cain't talk me out of Eva!"

"Yes! You give me a pain!" stated Mace. "Don't you think I've got any sense? She's a pretty girl, all right, but her old man is rich. And more'n that, he's pisen mean. The feller that named them the Strychnine Outfit knowed exactly what he was talking about. I tell you they're bad medicine to monkey with. We thought we'd be smart and beat their wagon out of two-bits and throw old Gilhooly down the well, and the next thing we knowed we woke up in jail—and came mighty near going to the Pen. Play along if you want to, but count me out, from now on. I know when I've got enough."

"Oh, there she is again!" gasped Little Joe as he caught a flash of white down the street. But Bowman turned aside into the swinging doors of the Long Horn and left him to chase will-o'-the-wisps alone. Yet as he sipped his cold tea in celebration of victory his mind went back to that same flash of white and he set down his glass with a sigh.

"Cramer," he said, "a man loses his nerve the minute he gets his eye on some girl. Or finds himself heading for the Pen. I feel like I'd been drug through a barb-wire fence—and all I get to drink is weak tea."

"Nevertheless," declared the barkeep, "it's the best thing for you. You can't drown your troubles in the flowing bowl—but who is this girl of yours?"

"I'm talking about Joe," corrected Long Rope. "He's chasing down the street after Eva. It's heading for the Pen that has got my nerve—that old Colonel is a hard-game sport."

"He is," admitted Cramer. "But we're going to break him, Mace. The NAI has just begun. I have hired a blackleg lawyer to begin that suit we spoke of for fifteen thousand dollars' damages. And fifteen thousand to him is fifteen thousand drops of blood, drawn away from his curmudgeon heart."

"Say, what are you talking about?" inquired Mace.

"Why, that suit for defamation of character. We will show him that a man's honor is beyond price.

“‘He who steals my purse steals trash
But he that filches from me my good name
Robs me of that which not enriches him,
And makes me poor indeed.’

“I will use that when I make my plea.”

Long Rope roused up suddenly and looked Cramer in the eye.

“You mean to say,” he demanded, “that you’re going to sue the Colonel—in my name?”

“Well, that was the understanding,” replied the barkeep. “And the money is as good as won. With a jury trial we could cinch that old scoundrel for a hundred thousand dollars, easy.”

“Yes, but I’ve got enough of telling funny stories. I don’t like that line, at all. And you know very well I was fooling! What the devil do I want to sue *him* for?”

“Why, defamation of character! Saying that you’re a cow-thief! Trying to railroad you into the Pen! Are you going to sit by and let that old rascal cast aspersions on your character?”

“Well—maybe not,” shrugged Mace. “But at the same time, Cramer, ain’t you getting kind of previous with this suit? Here I say in a joking way, like a man will when he’s won, that I’m going to sue for defamation of character. And a half an hour later you’ve hired some lawyer and got the case all lined out.”

“I’m a rapid worker, Mr. Bowman, when these moments of inspiration come. Did I fail you in the court room today? Didn’t I accomplish, with one answer to a question, what no high-priced lawyer could achieve? Didn't I prove my ability to sway Judge and jury alike, with one little human touch? Then why do you go back on me now?"

"I'm not going back on you, Cramer. But at the same time, dadburn it, I don't like that old courthouse and I don't want to monkey with Colonel Jones. That danged old reptile would have you killed for a nickel, and he's got me badly scared."

"*You* scared!" repeated Cramer. "Why, Mace, I must be mistaken, then. I've told every man in this town that you're the one hombre that is not afraid. I've been proud of you, my boy, and of the fearless manner in which you stood up for your rights. Defying his cook to collect at the wagon, throwing his bouncer down the bottomless well! What a night that was when at the NAI we voted you in, *cum laude!* You were battered and bruised, but your head was unbowed! You were master of your fate!"

"I sure tamed him!" admitted Mace. "And I beat McMullen, too. But there's something about this Penitentiary talk that certainly gets on my nerves."

"Yes, yes," soothed Cramer. "It has been a hard day for you. But all that's past—you have escaped their machinations. And now is the time to strike back! Without waiting a moment! Like the good fighter you are! Stand up for your rights and sue him for damages! And, sure as shooting, we'll win the whole fifteen thousand! Just that little hint, about spending all you win over the bar, is what set me off on the case.

Because this is a jury trial. If Jones wins the case, the jurors know they won't get a cent. But if *you* win, as you will, they know for a certainty that the drinks will be free for a month. Wine will flow like water—the whole town will be drunk! And think how Jonesy will swear!"

"Say, listen!" reasoned Bowman, "I'm a cowboy, see? And I don't like these trials, at all. Now you show me a steer, I don't care how big he is—"

"Aw, here!" spoke up Red Tutlow, who had been listening impatiently, "let me handle him, Brother Cramer."

He switched his brimming glass of whisky and Mace's glass of tea and nodded as Long Rope tossed it off.

"That's the stuff!" he pronounced approvingly. "This Western country would never be what it is if the old-timers had drunk nothing but tea. And whisky is like religion—a little of it don't hurt anybody."

"You're right," agreed Mace, pouring another one. "You can't expect a man to climb up on a bronk as long as he's got any *brains*. But with a few drinks under his belt he ain't afraid of all hell, to say nothing of this tinhorn, Jones."

"You said it!" nodded Tutlow. "I agree with you, perfectly. You've got a head like a tack—your remarks show the greatest perspicacity. W'y, Mace, you've got more sense when you're drunk than any man in this town when he's sober. The drunker you get the better your brains work. Now take that bronk-riding, where we win all their money. Who was it that slipped you a drink?

"It was me, eh? I knew you would win. I was backing you all the time to take first place in that steer-tying and I bet my whole roll you'd ride Elsie. You're a winner, Túcumcari. You come from a town where a coward and a weakling can't live. That's why I say we're going to trim old Colonel Jones and win this fifteen thousand, hands down.

"And then next fall, if they haven't had enough, I'm going to back you myself to beat Tex McMullen, tying ten steers to his one. I've got five thousand dollars on deposit with Cramer that says you can do it, anytime—each man to pick the other man's steers. And we'll save ten thousand out of this fifteen thousand damage money to bet on the side against Jones. Then we'll have the damnedest contest that the West has ever seen, right here in Pioneer Park! Are you on? Well, all right then—shake hands!"

Long Rope shook, nodding proudly as Red rehearsed his victories. Then as Cramer filled his glass he glanced at him curiously and remembered the suit against Jones.

"That'll be all right," he said negligently. "You can file them damage papers anytime."

CHAPTER XIX LITTLE JOE'S PARTY

THE summer went by with its ups and downs as Joe and Long Rope followed the Rodeos. Sometimes they won and sometimes not, but Little Joe had lost heart. He was always inquiring about Western Shows, which was touring on a circuit of its own, and his work in the arena fell off. Day-money, or second or third in the Calf Roping, was the most he expected to get; but Mace went in for Steer Roping and Bronk Riding and matched himself against the best.

He had a pair of spurs, a pair of shaps and a beaver hat that said he was the Champion Everything—and then, of course, the shirt. Wherever he rode in the grand parade that cloth-of-gold shirt with the purple *fleur-de-lis* set him off like the King of the World. And he was never too busy, when envious punchers stood at gaze, to relate how the shirt was won. But early in September his round of triumph was cut short by news from Western Shows. Little Eva and her mother had gone back to Bottomless Spring after a falling-out with Colonel Jones, and Joe was in a fever to follow.

Mace argued and reasoned, but at last he gave in and one hot day they rode west on the old Dry Trail. The level plains lay behind them—they were lost in the endless rolls, like a great sea frozen, waves and all—and as mile after mile fell behind them the pardners began to spit dry.

"Seems to me," observed Mace for the hundredth time, "we ought to see that monument. You don't reckon, Joe, we're lost?"

"A man is always lost on these Staked Plains," said Joe. "But *I know it*—we ought to be there."

"Well, that's what I say," agreed Bowman. "I came over this trail last spring. It was right out in here somewhere that I ran across the round-up and turned off to get a drink at the wagon."

"Say! Talk about a drink!" smacked Little Joe. "I could empty that bottomless spring. But I suppose old Gilhooly will be right there to see we don't drink too much."

"I wish that big stiff would drop dead!" complained Mace. "If it wasn't for him I'd be up in Pendleton, winning first place in steer-tying and everything. But nope, you had to go back to Eva—and I had to tag along, to throw this Gilhooly down the well. The first yip I hear out of him I'm going to soak him, good."

"Well, we'll be there pretty soon," spoke up Barfoot hopefully. "That is, unless we're lost. I'd swear I know every turn of this trail—but where in the world is that monument?"

They toiled up a long rise, their horses too dry to sweat, the dust crusted deep on their gaunt flanks; and then at the top they both reined in at once, for Bottomless Spring lay before them. There was the water-hole, the meadow, the house on the hill—but the monument itself was gone!

"What the devil!" exclaimed Joe. "If they haven't

tore it down to build that big, white warehouse! *Here's* where it used to stand—right here—and there ain't a rock of it left! Well, don't that beat the Dutch!"

"It sure does!" agreed Mace, stepping off his horse, "But right now we're going to start another one, I don't care if I am spitting cotton!"

He gathered up some scattered rocks and was putting them in a pile when from the swale below a hoarse voice bellowed up at them. It was Gilhooly, the fighting blacksmith.

"Be arf from there!" he roared; and with a muttered oath Bowman swung up on his horse and charged. Little Joe came clattering after him, but he stopped at the spring to drink. Mace leapt off of Jug and kept on.

"Were you talking to me?" he hollered, "you shanty-Irish baboon? Just wait till I get my hands on you and I'll shove that blat down your throat!"

"Oh! So it's you, sir!" cried the blacksmith, dodging back inside his newly built lodge. And Mace saw that it had been made from the monument.

"W'y, you dadburned whelp!" he raged. "Are you the man that tore down the rock-pile? We mighty near got lost, looking around for that monument—and here you've used it for a house."

"Oh, no, sir!" protested Gilhooly, "I hadn't a thing to do with it. The Colonel ordered it down just before he left home. We needed the stone for a warehouse."

"Just wait till I get a drink," promised Mace, "and I'll tie one of them stones around your neck. Can you beat that?" he hollered to Joe in a voice that reached to the hills, "they've tore down the monument for a warehouse!"

He sank down and drank deep from the crystal spring, then strode back and confronted Gilhooly.

"So you're back on the job, eh?" he taunted. "Keeping lost men from finding the spring! Well, put up your dukes, you ugly man's dog—I can lick you with one hand!"

He threw off his hat, but as he advanced on the blacksmith a voice called down from the house.

"Yoo-hoo! Come on up, boys! You don't need to fight!"

"But I *want* to fight!" answered back Long Rope, walking closer. "Are you the yap that hollered: 'Be arf with you!' a minute ago?"

"Well, yis, I am now," admitted Gilhooly. "But I didn't know it was you. Miss Eva is calling, sir, so you're welcome to pass through the gate."

"Go ahead, Joe," said Mace, "I'll be along later, after I've settled with Mr. Gilhooly. I feel just like knocking this big bull's horns off and throwing him in with the stray-herd."

There was a patter of feet down the long, winding path that led from the house on the hill and Little Eva appeared at the gate. Her yellow curls were dancing, her blue eyes bright with laughter; and at sight of her Bowman lowered his hands.

"I thought I heard a familiar voice," she said. "And it's a lucky thing for Gilhooly. Are you fighting again?" she chided, making eyes at him reproachfully. "What a terrible man you are!"

"Well, don't I have to lick him to get that—er—reward?" asked Mace. And they both laughed, while she shook her head.

"I'm grown up now," she said, glancing coquettishly at Little Joe, "and there won't be any more rewards. And besides I'm in disgrace. So won't you please come up—and say nothing about it? That's Mother, out on the porch."

"Wait till I tie my horse up," evaded Long Rope; but Eva only clapped her hands.

"Take care of those horses," she called to a roustabout, and led them reluctantly to the house.

It was big and broad, made of white stone with red facings and with a wide porch facing the east; and there, staring anxiously, stood Little Eva's mother, the redoubtable Merry Hart. She was a small woman, but dark, and with eyes so piercing and steady they seemed to bore holes like bullets.

"Good evening, boys," she said. "Come in and sit down. I'm sorry you had trouble with Gilhooly."

"Oh, that's all right," bowed Mace, "no trouble at all, Mrs. Jones. But if you don't mind I'll stay outside."

"Very well," she answered quietly. But as she glanced at Joe he capitulated and passed inside.

"Oh, do come!" implored Eva, looking back through the door; but Bowman shook his head doggedly.

"No," he answered, "this is Little Joe's party. And besides, I'm kind of hot, anyhow."

"Oh, about the monument?" she asked. "I hope you're not mad at me, too!"

"Nope," he shrugged. "I reckon you didn't do it. Go on in and talk to Joe."

She glanced back over her shoulder to where her mother and Barfoot were settling down in their chairs, then she closed the door behind her impulsively and sat down with him on the porch.

"I'll stay out and entertain you," she promised virtuously. "How did you come to get back so soon?"

"Oh, Joe heard you were home—and I had to come along to get him past Gilhooly."

"And didn't you come to see *me* at all?" she asked. "After I'd crowned you King, and everything!"

"Nope," he said. "If I'd had my way I'd he up at Pendleton, right now, showing them Oregon boys how to rope."

She gazed at him a minute and then laughed, doubtfully.

"You're always making jokes," she said. "Does Mr. Barfoot think so much of me?"

"Oh, yes," he answered. "Don't think of nothing else."

"Well, why?" she demanded at length.

"We-ell," he began, looking her over appraisingly, "of course you're a mighty pretty girl. Got 'em all crazy, as far as that goes. But what ketches Joe, you're little and can't pat him on the head."

"What—really?" she cried, making eyes at him.

"That's right," he said, "he don't want no tall girl,

because the first time she wanted to tease him she'd reach down and rumple his hair. With me, now, it's just the other way."

"You mean," she quavered, "that you like tall girls best?"

"That's right," he responded soberly. "Little girls are all right for little fellers like Joe. But me, I like a big, strong, upstanding girl—one that can hit a bull between the eyes with her fist and knock him to his knees."

Eva stared at him for a moment as if doubting her own ears, then she dashed away a tear and laughed.

"I—I thought you meant it!" she said.

"Oh, no!" he protested, suddenly relenting and patting the hand he found in his, "I never meant nothing, of course. Or that is—well, maybe I did. But say, your mother is going to come out and scold you if you don't go in with the company."

Eva twisted uneasily and took her hand away.

"You are always making jokes," she sighed. "But don't you like little girls—if they're strong?"

"Well," he began, with a fatherly smile, "little girls are mighty cute, of course. But that's just the trouble—they'll always have their own way. Never knew it to fail that a little woman could wrap a big man around her finger—and that's awful humiliating to a man."

"You might get used to it, and like it!" she suggested; and reached out for his hand again.

"Well, maybe," he conceded. "But another thing I

can't stand is a big, tall man like your father. Always bossing you around and crabbing about a cent—"

"But he *isn't* my father!" she protested. "My father died when I was a little baby, so Mother married *him.* But I feel just like you do—I hate him! And when I came home and found the monument torn down I—I cried!"

"Never mind!" he soothed, "we all know it ain't your fault. And I'm sure glad he isn't your old man. Because when I get back to town I'm going to sue Colonel Jones for fifteen thousand dollars."

"What—Daddy?" she cried. "Why, what for?"

"For telling everybody I was a cow-thief. I'm suing for defamation of character."

"And do you expect to win?" she inquired.

"Sure!" he said. "And that ain't nothing! Before I get through with him I'm going to run him plumb out of the country!"

"But why?" she demanded, startled.

"Well—to get rid of Tex McMullen," he hazarded a a venture.

Little Eva settled back and gazed up at him coquetishly.

"So that's it!" she exclaimed, sighing rapturously. "What a funny man you are! I *never* know when you're joking!"

"Yes, but I'm not joking," he said.

"Well," she began, "Tex is a wonderful roper, but—"

"He ain't no roper at all! I can beat him with one hand!"

"Can you really, Mr. Bowman?"

"Sure can, and I've got a thousand dollars to prove it. After I win this fifteen thousand from the Colonel I'll put half of that up, too. For a challenge match, you know."

He threw out his chest and nodded at her arrogantly and Eva sought to puncture his pride.

"Of course," she began, "I admire a good roper. But there are other qualities in a man that a woman notices more. Some like them kind of modest and shy."

"I've noticed that, too," parried Bowman. "Take Little Joe now—that's what makes him so popular. He's got more friends than any man in the country."

"Yes, but Daddy says he's part Indian," she confided.

"So are the Randolphs, of Virginia—all descended from Pocahontas. The proudest family in the State. And this here Comanche blood ain't ordinary Injun blood at all. All the best people around El Toro are part Comanche. Only wish I had some Injun blood myself."

"But—but Daddy says he's a cow-thief!"

"Yes, and he says *I'm* a cow-thief, too. That's exactly what I'm suing him for. When you say that, you've got to prove it—a man's good name is *property.* You just wait till the fall term of court begins and see what the jury says! If it hurts him as much to give up fifteen thousand dollars as it does to give a cowboy a square meal, your Old Man is due to die."

"Oh, but he isn't my Old Man," she protested tearfully. "And I just hate his charging for meals. But he's not here now, so Mother and I want you both to stay for supper."

"Not me!" pronounced Mace. "I won't eat the grub of a man that calls me a cow-thief. Mighty nice of you to invite us, and we sure appreciate the honor, but Joe and me have got our pride. Haven't we, Joe?" he demanded as Barfoot came out, closely followed by Merry Hart.

"I don't know what you're talking about," grumbled Little Joe; and Bowman could see he was hacked.

"Well, answer for yourself," he said. "Miss Eva was inviting us to supper."

"All right," agreed Joe, brightening up.

"But I told her—for myself—that I wouldn't go into the house of a man that had called me a cow-thief. I like a good fight—and a good fighter—but the Colonel has crowded me too far."

"Oh now, Mr. Bowman," protested Merry Hart politely. "He's very hot-tempered, as you know. I'm sure you'd be very welcome if you would consent to stay—and Mr. Barfoot, too."

She bowed, but rather grimly, to poor, embarrassed Joe and Little Eva made a final plea; but Bowman was suddenly adamant.

"Nope," he said, "I'm suing the Colonel for defamation of character. And being as you ladies are under his wing I'll have to bid you good-by. Come down to the trial on the first of October and see the legal battle of the century."

He shook hands soberly with Merry Hart and her pouting daughter and strode off down the path alone. But before he had got his horse Joe Barfoot came running after him and they rode out the gate together.

"Good-by!" called Little Eva. "Come again—and stay longer!"

She was standing on the porch waving her hand, but only Little Joe waved back.

CHAPTER XX WELCOME HOME!

IT was not much of a party for Little Joe Barfoot, for after riding hundreds of miles to call on Eva she had stayed outside to talk with Mace. He had sat with Merry Hart, who was not feeling very merry, for the briefest period that could pass for a call; and then, when they had come out, Bowman had picked a quarrel and gone off and left him alone. So there was nothing to do but tag along after him, but Joe was packing a grouch.

"You're a jim dandy—you are!" he railed as they rode off to the west. "So you cain't even eat the Colonel's grub, and him up in Canada somewhere! They didn't know a thing about that suit you brought against him, but of course you had to bring it up. And then, when we was starving, you made a long speech and bid the ladies good-by! Why couldn't you keep your mouth shut and gimme a chance with Eva? I'd've stayed for supper, and glad to!"

"Next time," said Mace, "you make your own calls. I'm through with trying to help you. That little girl stepped out on you, and the next thing I know you'll be claiming I'm trying to steal her."

"I wouldn't put it past you," grumbled Joe.

"I was listening for that, but you saw her first, Joe. And you can't say I tried to snare her. But after this, just to show that I'm strictly on the square, you can pull off your courting lone-handed. You heard my sentiments about tearing down that monument—and I'm suing the Colonel, anyhow. But if you feel different, and want to keep your welcome, you can stay out of this civil suit."

"Well, if you don't mind then," sighed Barfoot, "I will. And if you're going to town I believe I'll stop off and see how my ranch is getting on. It ain't far, anyway—and maybe in a day or two I can go back and see Eva again."

"O.K.," agreed Mace, "and the best of luck to you." And at the fork of the trails they parted.

Little Joe rode north towards the lonely ranch which he had left in the care of a hand; but Bowman plugged steadily on until, long after dark, he crossed the bridge into gay El Toro. Never before had he seen a town quite so lively, quite so full of good fellowship and grim jokes. Not six months before, he had crossed that same bridge on the way to the County Jail and El Toro had not looked quite so good. But when James G. Cramer had appeared on the horizon his woes had miraculously disappeared.

The magnificent diamond in his broad expanse of shirt had lit up their cell like a star. It had shone forth as a symbol of affluence and good will, and of faith in his fellow-man. And since that day Long Rope's life had been changed and made both spectacular and successful. From an obscure contest rider he had become within a month the Champion Steer Roper of the World. He had won honors and acclaim and Tex McMullen's fancy shirt—even the friendship of Eva Jones.

He had kept it from Joe, but Little Eva was more than a friend.

She had a look in her eye that left him vaguely uneasy when he remembered that she was really Joe's girl. And when he did not, as had happened several times, it made him kind of crazy, like Joe.

She seemed the only woman in the world. Her eyes were like stars, her smile a magic spell, her hands slender tendrils that clutched his heart. And when he sought to evade her, to hand her back to Joe, she laid hold of him with a will all her own. She made him a traitor to his friend—to Little Joe, the man who was his pardner. That was why, when he escaped her presence, he had not even looked back.

But now the die was cast, he had renounced even her friendship, and this civil suit against the man she called Daddy would set them apart forever. It was a declaration of war. But war was what he wanted, after that tragic night in jail when his very life had seemed at an end. Before him there had loomed years of solitude and imprisonment, with the stamp of a convict on his brow—and all to feed the vanity and sate the revenge of this showman, Colonel Jones. Was fifteen thousand dollars too much to ask to wipe out the memory of that night?

Mace slept in the corral where Brown Jug munched his hay, but in the morning the stableman recognized him and El Toro welcomed him home. It was heart-warming, after months among strangers, to be taken to the heart of a whole town. The drinks were set up royally at the Long Horn bar, Phat Noland and Red Tutlow hurried in; while before the great mirror with its array of gleaming glasses James G. Cramer regarded him affectionately.

"Back again!" he declaimed, "and thrice welcome. Now the great work of improving North America can go on!"

"You mean," suggested Tutlow, "throwing the hooks into Colonel Jones! Set 'em up, boys! The drinks are on me."

He was his old carefree self, but the glassy stare had left his eyes and the barkeep poured out a strange drink. It was sparkling white and as clear as snow-water, and Long Rope regarded it curiously.

"What's this?" he asked at last, as Red filled up again; and the Champion Booze Fighter grinned.

"This is—er—water!" he announced, "my new drink. I'm on the wagon now. Say, come over here and I'll tell you all about it. You're the only man in town that doesn't know."

He laid hold of Mace and led him to a chair while the curious gathered around to listen again.

"Funniest story you ever heard," began Red. "I took the cure—last spring. My sister made me do it—she thinks a whole lot of me—and that preacher that's making love to her. They told me it was my duty to my numerous friends, and my heart was feeling the strain, so I told 'em: All right, I'd go. But not to trust me with any money on the road or I'd spend every dollar for hooch. So the day before I started I went the rounds of the saloons, saying good-by to all the bartenders; and every one of them gave me a full quart bottle to cheer me on my way.

"They were all down at the station to see me off when the preacher called me over to one side and slipped me a six-ounce bottle of rye. He said the doctor had advised him it was dangerous to stop entirely, and I could use this to taper off on. Well, he was a good sport anyhow, and going to marry my sister, so I thanked him and got on the train. But my entire overcoat was full of quart bottles, so I managed to get along.

"At Kansas City I was met by another preacher that my sister's friend had wired to; and so, between them all, I got to the sanitarium O.K. I'd drunk it all up, thinking it was the last I'd ever get; but the first thing that doctor did was to set out a big full bottle! It's a fact—he gave me all I wanted. Then he shot some black stuff into my arm and told me to have a good time.

"Well, we went to the theater and had a grand time; but on the morning of the eighth day when I got up to take my eye-opener, I had to spit it out. Couldn't swallow it—it tasted terrible. I thought sure it was doped, but it wasn't. *All whisky* tastes that way now. I'm on the wagon for life!"

He laughed and ordered the drinks, but Mace could see that his sister had been right. The whisky had burned him out—his skin was dry, his voice husky—but the glaze over his eyes was gone.

"Well, come on!" he said, when the big welcome was over and the crowd had drifted away, "let's go into the back room and talk over this lawsuit that's going to improve North America. What do we care, boys, where the Gulf Stream flows, as long as we can cinch Colonel Jones!"

"It seems," observed Cramer, as he sank into his chair, "almost a profanation of the high purpose of our great company to concentrate all our energies on Jones. It makes my hot Southern blood boil every time I think of this miserable circus-man, posing and riding and pretending to be a cowboy. A Westerner, if you please, and charging for meals at his wagon! But you are right, Brother Tutlow! Let the Gulf Stream flow where it will, even if it warms the cold bosom of Ireland, where all the policemen come from. We are after the man who employs one Gilhooly to carry out his tyrant will. As a committee of three, to resist all oppression, I move we go into executive session."

He pressed the button and after the drinks were served spread a mass of papers on the table.

"Here are the briefs and records," he began, "of this blackleg lawyer I have employed. If he should plead the case himself it would be thrown out of court before he had lost his first wind. Like all of them, he takes the sign for the thing symbolized, the symbol for the substance. But we have learned, Brother NAIs, that there is something above the law. All the papers and pleas in the world are nothing. The will of the people is supreme. That is why, with your permission, I wish to plead this case myself, although I feel that my reputation is at stake.

"Colonel Jones is very indignant that he should be summoned into court, cutting short his season on the road to answer to a charge like this. He has retained two expensive outside lawyers to seek out each technical mistake. But fortunately for us, Judge Henshaw will preside; and with him on the bench we need fear no miscarriage of justice. He is telling that maverick story everywhere. A gentleman from El Paso who passed through the other day informs me it's the joke of the town."

"That was a good one," laughed Long Rope. "Have you got another one to spring at this trial?"

"Well—perhaps!" replied the barkeep modestly. "I depend upon the inspiration of the moment. We were confronted then with a desperate situation which called for a desperate expedient. But in this case, Colonel Jones is in the position of the defendant, with public opinion arrayed against him and a jury of twelve men as his judges. Our ace in the hole is the one you suggested—that the damages awarded shall be spent over the Long Horn bar.

"The El Toro County men, as you know, are generous to a fault and the Colonel is a miserly curmudgeon. It will appeal to the sense of humor of the jury to see him mulcted to buy the drinks for the town. Just let that rumor spread and our case is won, no matter what his lawyers may say. I am counting the days until the first of October, when the Colonel must appear in court. What a guilty, hangdog look he will have when he faces these men and reads his fate in their eyes. And there is nothing in the law to hinder the plaintiff from spending his damages over the bar. The only question is—how much?"

"Well, not too much!" suggested Tutlow, "or the whole town will have to take the cure. I think a general statement that the drinks will be free will be enough to swing the jury. Because they know very well that if the Colonel wins he won't even buy a drink for himself.

"But here's something, boys, that we don't want to overlook. We've got another Rodeo coming and we can make it the greatest event in the West. Now let's divide the money like this. One half of the damages to be spent over the bar. The other half goes into a war-chest, to nick the Hash-knives again. I'll never be satisfied until Mace and Tex McMullen are matched for that Steer Roping Contest, for the Championship of the World. That would be a big drawing card that would bring thousands of people, and I believe that Bowman can win. So I move we get behind him with the whole damage war-chest and laugh these Hash-knives out of town."

"How about it, Brother Bowman?" inquired Cramer. "Do you think you can beat Tex again?"

"I know it!" declared Mace. "And I'll tell you why—he's yellow! Did you see him last spring when he took after that big steer? He was afraid of him—and afraid of his short rope. That's why I've made my brace and I'll make it again—that I can rope ten steers to his one. I'll get a steer so fierce he'll never dare to tie to it! And I'll tackle any steer in the world!"

"That's the talk!" barked Red, starting up. "That's what I've been saying, all summer. If we back Mace on this play we've got that gang beat. They're tin-horns, every one of them, and like all short sports they'll bet their shirt on what they think is a sure thing. Ten to one—that's big odds! And Tex won first money again, at Cheyenne. But I'd just like to ask Mace one question—where are you going to get that steer?"

"Easy!" laughed Long Rope. "I've got him all spotted—down in Mexico. Ever hear of Matador? He's the biggest steer in the State of Chihuahua, and he's killed three Mexicans that I know of. They had him in the bull-ring until he got so *bravo* that none of the matadors would fight him. So they stagged him and put him out on the big Terrazas ranch, where they're holding him for a thousand dollars—gold!"

"Go and buy him!" rapped out Red, "and we've got these rascals skinned! Why didn't you say so, before?"

"I was waiting," said Mace. "That's all."

"Well, don't breathe a word of it," warned Cramer. "It's the sense of the meeting that we purchase this man-killer, put him in the ring with Tex, and bet the whole roll on the steer. All in favor? The meeting is adjourned."

CHAPTER XXI
DEFAMATION OF CHARACTER

THE El Toro court room was crowded to the doors when Long Rope's suit for damages began, for a rumor had spread like wildfire that if he won the drinks would be free. He was suing Colonel Jones as a matter of principle and the damages would be spent over the bar. Day and night, for weeks and months, until the last dollar was gone—for a man's good name is *property!*

There were some who sensed a joke in this demand for good hard dollars in compensation for being called a cow-thief, but neither Bowman nor his attorney nor his special pleader, James G. Cramer, were seen to crack a smile. They sat solemnly at their table on the right; and Colonel Jones sat grim and distant on the left; with two high-priced lawyers from Santa Fe.

The Judge came in and laid off his robes with more than his usual severity but as his eyes met those of

Long Rope they lit up with the ghost of a smile. Then the long-winded allegations of Bowman's attorney were read, while Cramer gazed at the ceiling. The lawyers tangled in a wordy battle, in which the attorneys from Santa Fe noted an exception to every adverse ruling and Cramer's shyster barked like a dog, and still the mastermind dreamt on. The jury was drawn, twelve good men and true, and he did not challenge a man. But when the fact had been proved by competent witnesses that Jones had called Bowman a cow-thief, the great man rose to his feet.

"Your Honor," he began, "and gentlemen of the jury. I have listened, as have you, to the arguments of the attorneys who have been engaged to present this case. The attorney for the plaintiff has attempted to prove that his good name has been irreparably damaged, while the learned gentlemen who represent the defendant have denied *in toto* everything which reflected on their client. That is what they are paid for, and I make no complaint; but at the same time it is evident that, had they been engaged by the other side, white would be black and black white.

"But I come before you, gentlemen, not as a hired protagonist, equally willing to defend either side. I come as a friend of the court and the plaintiff, a sort of *amicus curiae,* whose sole interest is to see justice done. I am not a lawyer, nor do I understand the legal quibblings you have heard. All I know is that my friend has suffered a grievous wrong by being called, and repeatedly, a cow-thief.

"Now that is a name which, among friends, can be bandied to and fro. But when, as in this case, there is malice behind the act, it violates an ancient human right. Every man is entitled to defend his good name. It is property—his dearest possession. For what says William Shakespeare, the Bard of Avon, than whom a greater poet never lived:

" 'Good name in man and woman, dear my lord,
Is the immediate jewel of their souls:
Who steals my purse steals trash; 'tis something, nothing;
'Twas mine, 'tis his, and has been slave to thousands:
But he that filches from me my good name,
Robs me of that which not enriches him,
And makes me poor indeed.' "

He paused and glanced at the jury, who regarded him with a new-found awe; and across at the frowning defendant, who gave him a poisonous look.

"This, my friends," he went on, "is not such a case as we saw tried here a few months ago. And yet it goes back to that case. The same malice, the same enmity, lies behind. In that case the defendant, Colonel Jones, registered a criminal charge against the plaintiff. He claimed that Mr. Bowman had, unlawfully and with malice aforethought, stolen one of his yearling calves; in which case, if the allegation had been proved, he would now be free to call him a cow-thief. But the jury, without leaving their seats, declared that Mace Bowman was innocent of any intent to commit a crime. It was proved that at the time the said calf was killed Mr. Bowman's mind was a blank."

A sudden shout of laughter from the court room was silenced by the bailiff's hammer, but the audience sat back with a sigh. They had come there to see Cramer make a monkey of the Colonel and at last he was beginning to perform. Jones went into a huddle with his two attorneys, who both objected at once, and then the barkeeper went on.

"That case, Your Honor and gentlemen of the jury, was in the criminal court, and the plaintiff's liberty was in jeopardy. But when a jury of his peers adjudged him 'Not Guilty' the status of my young friend changed. He became a free man, his good name was restored to him, his unjustified arrest was rebuked. And when Colonel Jones dared again to call him a cow-thief he laid himself liable to the law.

"This is a civil suit for damages, for defamation of character, in the amount of fifteen thousand dollars. But let no man think, as has been intimated by my opponents, that it is an attempt to bleed their client. Colonel Jones is a rich man. There lies beneath his land inexhaustible stores of oil. His cattle are numbered into the thousands. But does that give him the right to call a man a cow-thief—unless he can *prove* him a thief? Most certainly not, and Mr. Bowman, as a matter of principle, has brought this suit for damages. Not one dollar of the award which we so confidently expect to receive is asked to enrich the plaintiff, although he has suffered a deep wrong. It is to punish the defendant and teach him, once for all, that a man's good name is priceless.

"We have here, gentlemen of the jury, a humble cowboy—although the Champion Steer Roper of the World—bringing suit against a millionaire. An oil magnate, if you wish—a man of boundless acres which he assumes to rule like a king. On that broad expanse of land he will brook no opposition. His word is law among the minions who do his will, but our friend here dared to oppose him.

"When he came to the Hash-knife wagon, where the employees of the defendant demanded pay before he could eat, he made bold to flout such parsimony. And when he came to Bottomless Spring, that oasis of the Staked Plains, his righteous indignation burst forth. He seized the hired bouncer of the defendant, who attempted to drive him away, and cast him, anvil and all, down the well. It was the first blow against oppression and tyranny."

The attorneys for Colonel Jones leapt up both at once to register the customary objections, and their objections were as perfunctorily sustained; but at the mention of Gilhooly a great guffaw swept the crowd. Only James G. Cramer and the Judge upon the bench preserved an unsmiling countenance.

"You may laugh, friends," went on Cramer, "but Mr. Bowman paid dearly for his temerity. Not half an hour after this battle with the blacksmith he was arrested by the defendant and two cowboys. Despite his many wounds and his injured eye he was bound on the back of his horse and led like a criminal to town. But when he came before a jury, that great bulwark of the common people's rights, how quickly was all this changed! He was acquitted and his good name cleared!

"But Colonel Jones, far from accepting this rebuke, went forth upon the street and in the presence of many witnesses stated repeatedly that the plaintiff was a cow-thief. He denounced the verdict as a travesty of justice, and expressed the belief that a certain jesting remark had made the jury forget its oath. But I maintain that the plaintiff's definition of a maverick—"

"I object!" shouted Colonel Jones's attorney; and Cramer bowed to the ruling of the court.

"Very well, Your Honor," he said. "Let us stick to the case at hand. The defendant has practically admitted that he called Mr. Bowman a cow-thief, and we have proved it by competent witnesses. But he has brought forth no evidence to prove theft, and I challenge him to do so now. Avoiding this line, he has chosen instead to minimize the damage to the plaintiff, to intimate that to a cowboy, earning forty dollars a month, fifteen thousand dollars' damages is exorbitant.

"I call your attention, gentlemen, to what I said before—that a matter of principle is involved. To a humble cowboy the amount might indeed seem large. But to the man who pays, it is so small that it sinks into insignificance. This is not a suit to enrich the plaintiff but to punish the defendant for his malice. It is to warn him that wealth and power mean nothing before a jury of his peers.

"Now before I close the case for the plaintiff, I wish to call a few witnesses to testify concerning his character. If he is, as has been intimated, a man of low principles, the damage to his good name is negligible. But if, as I maintain, he is a man of the highest character, a man loved and honored by all who know him; then fifteen thousand dollars is not a cent too much to compensate him for this defamation of character. I will call Neil Monroe to the stand."

He smiled as the merchant came forward and testified to the high character of Bowman; and then, one after the other, he called on Tutlow and Phat Noland and the leading citizens of the town. But all the time as he listened his eyes searched through the crowd that stood at the back of the room, and as a slim little figure slipped in and sat down he held up his hand dramatically.

"Your Honor," he said, "and gentlemen of the jury, I am going to call one more witness and ask that witness one question. And with that I will close my case. I see in the audience a little lady whom we all know and admire. Miss Eva Jones! Will you please step to the front?"

He bowed and smiled as, looking very small, Little Eva came up the aisle and took her seat in the chair. She blushed and went pale and blushed again as she glanced uncertainly about, but when she saw Mace at the table below her she bit her lip and looked away. Then she raised her hand and took the oath, while the audience sat hushed and still.

"Miss Jones," began Cramer, "you are called as a witness to the moral character of the plaintiff, Mace Bowman. Do you think he would steal a calf?"

"Oh, no!" cried Little Eva; and once more her tall questioner bowed.

"That is all," he said. "I thank you." And Eva stepped down and fled.

Then for two long hours the lawyers from Santa Fe volleyed and thundered and spouted forth eloquence; but the jury had made up their minds.

When the smoke cleared away they gave a verdict for the plaintiff in the sum of fifteen thousand dollars.

CHAPTER XXII A GOOD SKATER

VESUVIUS in eruption was nothing but a smoke-signal to the way Colonel Jones raved and cursed. He gave off at the head like a switchman, but the will of the jury was supreme. For the good of his soul, and to punish him for his arrogance, they had assessed him the full fifteen thousand; and at eight shots to the dollar that would buy the stupendous total of a hundred and twenty thousand drinks.

There was a rush from the court room to the Long Horn Saloon where the big bottles were set out along the bar, and with every round they drank confusion to Colonel Jones and long life to the Champion of the World. And, not to be outdone, Mace stood in the midst of them and drank cold tea for hours. The crust of his enemy had been broken like the back of a hard-shelled crab. He had learned at last what the common people thought of him, and that a good man's name was *property*.

But one thing worried Long Rope and after the first mad carouse he requested a private interview with Cramer.

"Well," he began, "you certainly knocked the bung out, as far as the booze is concerned. But here are you and me and Red, all riding the water-wagon, while the rest of the town gets drunk. There's going to be a rush to take the gold-cure if this celebration runs its course; but what I want to know, Mr. Cramer, is how come Little Eva was called. Did you depend upon the inspiration of the moment, or was it all framed in advance?"

"My dear young friend," reasoned the barkeep, "why go behind the returns?

> " 'If all the world be worth thy winning,
> Think, oh think it worth enjoying:
> Lovely Thais sits beside thee,
> Take the good the gods provide thee.' "

"Well, sure," responded Mace, "but what has that got to do with the case? We set out to tap the

Colonel, but was it absolutely necessary to ring in his charming daughter? He gave her a black look when she okayed my character. And besides, there's Little Joe!"

"Yes? What about him?" inquired Cramer.

"Well, Eva is his girl—he claims he saw her first!"

"The greatest fallacy in the world!" sighed the barkeeper. "As if a woman could be claimed by right of discovery, and located, like a gold mine! But I tell you, young man, there is no right to a woman's heart except it be given by her. Kings, potentates and powers may rise and fall, but woman is woman still."

"All right," agreed Long Rope, "if you say so. But that ain't answering my question. Did you take advantage of that poor little girl to get her in wrong with her father—"

"Not at all!" broke in Cramer, with a knowing smile. "Since you must know, she asked to be called."

"The hell you say!" burst out Bowman, astounded. "Did she turn against her Old Man?"

"He is only her father by adoption—and love will find a way."

"Say, what are you hinting at and quoting poetry about?" demanded Mace. "You've got me in bad with Joe!"

"That's his misfortune," smiled Cramer. "The lady is in love with you. Every man on that jury read the story at a glance, and right there our case was won."

"Pretty slick, pretty slick," nodded Mace. "But where do I get off, now? What am I going to say to Joe when I go out to his ranch again? We were figuring on catching Whistling Rufus!"

"You may say what you will," responded the barkeep. "There's no getting around the facts. And which is more important—the love of that radiant young creature or the possession of an outlaw bronk?"

"That ain't it!" protested Bowman. "Little Joe and me are pardners and I don't want to take away his girl. And another thing, Cramer, when he hears about this case, Joe is going to give me fits."

"Very likely," answered Cramer. "But I'm no father-confessor. Nor am I competent to give advice to young lovers, having failed at the game myself. But get out of town, boy, until this drinking bout is over, and let your conscience be your guide."

"Say!" observed Long Rope. "There was a cracking good preacher spoiled when they let you become a barkeep. But all the same, Brother Cramer, I'm going to take your advice and get out of town, right now."

"But don't forget," warned Cramer, "the improvement of North America! There's five thousand dollars on deposit in my safe to back you in that contest with Tex!"

"Leave it to me!" promised Mace. "He's back with the wagon." And with a wink and a laugh he was gone.

Brown Jug hit the trail at a gallop and kept on the run for miles. It was that which made him strong and kept up his wind, and he too had felt shut up in the town; but when at last they came to the road that turned off to Joe's ranch, Mace pulled him down to a walk. They had come a long way and he had had lots of time to think, but what would he say to Joe? Should he tell the truth and take a cussing, or say nothing and let him find out?

He was still pondering on the problem when at a turn of the trail he came to the Barfoot ranch. It was a stick-and-mud house at the base of the hill, not far from a half-dry lake with a barrel up-ended in the mire. The barrel supplied the water, and the cattle that came to drink kept Joe and his hired man in beef. But as a home to which to bring the daughter of a millionaire it did not appeal to Mace.

The two-roomed house stood empty, its sagging door unlatched, but at sundown Joe and his helper returned. They threw their horses into the pasture, picked up their saddles without a word, and clumped wearily up to the house.

"Hello!" hailed Bowman, stepping out to meet them. "Been out on the round-up, Joe?"

"Nope! Range-branding!" he answered, apathetically. "How'd you come out on your lawsuit?"

"We won it," announced Mace, "for the full fifteen thousand. Every man in El Toro is on a drunk."

"Going to drink it all up?" inquired the gaunt old cowman who held down the ranch for Joe. "Well, say, I might go to town!"

"No hurry," laughed Long Rope, "there'll be plenty left. A feller figured out there would be a hundred and twenty thousand drinks, but Cramer is going to cut it short. When he thinks they've had enough he'll quit."

"That's lots of whisky," observed the old man wistfully; but Joe made no remarks. He had turned Indian —there was something on his mind.

"Where you going?" he asked at last, after they had eaten and stretched out to smoke. "Out to the ranch to see Little Eva?"

"Ump-umm!" denied Mace. "I'm heading the other way. Let's go down and catch Whistling Rufus!"

"Aw, what's the matter with you?" grumbled Barfoot. "I've got to work my ranch."

"Losing some?" inquired Bowman, after a silence, and Little Joe grunted assent. He was down in the dumps so Mace left him alone until, in the morning, he spoke.

"Let's go over to Bottomless Spring!" he proposed.

"What for?" demanded Long Rope bluntly. "Do you want to get me killed? You'd ought to have been in town and heard the Colonel give off head. He'd just about scalp me if we'd meet."

"Well, I need you," confessed Joe. "Ain't very welcome, myself. Every time I show my face I have a quarrel with Eva. Wants to know why *you* never come!"

"I told her—and told her mother—I wasn't coming any more; and you were right there and heard me. And now that I've soaked the Colonel for that fifteen thousand dollars I'd look pretty making a call!"

"All the same," insisted Barfoot, "I want you to come along. To tell you the truth, Gilhooly is on the warpath and won't let me past the gate."

"Aw, cripes," complained Long Rope, "what's the use of sticking around where we know we're nowise welcome? What chance have we got, either one of us, of winning a millionaire's daughter? She's a pretty girl, all right, and I get dizzy every time I look at her; but her father and her mother both hate me like a horny-toad and I haven't got a Chinaman's chance. So get on your horse and let's go down to Whisky Lake and snare old Whistling Rufus!"

"No!" snapped Joe. "You can ketch him if you want to, but I'm going back to see Eva. I don't see why you won't come along."

"Well, all right," agreed Mace, "if it makes any difference to you. But before we start I might as well tell you that Eva has got me going. I'm not trying to steal her, understand; but don't blame me if anything goes wrong. I'll put you past Gilhooly, if that's all you want—"

"All right!' " agreed Barfoot. "I've been over there twice and the rascal turned me back."

"I'll fix him," promised Bowman. "But it's no use, Joe. The Old Lady is dead set against us. You go up there now and she'll call you—proper!"

"I'm going!" declared Little Joe, stubbornly; and reluctantly Mace followed his lead.

It was a crisp October morning and their horses fought their heads until they let them out to a gallop, but as they neared the ranch a sound of lowing cattle made Long Rope rein up short.

"There's the round-up," he announced, "and Cramer

told me particularly to rib up a quarrel with Tex. Then bring up the matter of that contest and get him to cover the bet."

"You can do that going back," sulked Joe.

"No I can't," argued Mace. "He'll be in at the wagon now, or roping calves on the cutting-grounds. The big, swelled-up stiff, I'd like nothing better than to call him by his right name. There's dog blood in his family, if I'm any judge."

"Well, I'll go along with you," decided Little Joe, at last. "But don't you git into a fight, now!"

"Oh, no," responded Bowman, "but I'd just like to see if they're still charging two-bits for meals."

He turned off the road and galloped down a long swale towards the noise of the bellowing herd, but just as they sighted the cowboys at their work they passed the Hash-knife wagon. It was parked at the mouth of a little side canyon and Sowbelly Johnson was watching them.

"Aw, come on!" protested Barfoot, as Mace stopped, "and leave the old tarrapin alone."

"Nope," dissented Long Rope, "let's go over and say 'Howdy' and get a cup of coffee."

He rode up towards the wagon, left his horse with Joe, and walked in on the dour old cook.

"Good morning, Mister Johnson," he greeted. "How's everything? What's the good word?"

"They ain't none!" returned Sowbelly, "and if you want a cup of coffee, our charge is twenty-five cents."

"Oh, that's all right," nodded Bowman, picking up a big tin cup.

"In advance!" rasped the cook. "In advance!"

"I'm sorry, Cusi," jested Mace. "All I've got is a thousand dollar bill."

"Well," responded Johnson, his eyes lighting up, "give it to me—I reckon I can change it."

"Nope," answered Long Rope, "that ain't the way I work. You don't give me my meal until I pay you two-bits, and I don't give you my bill until you show me you've got the change."

"Here comes the Colonel!" warned Little Joe. "And Tex McMullen!" he added.

"Good!" pronounced Bowman, giving the cook a quarter and pouring out his cup of coffee; and when the circus-man rode up he was sitting down cross-legged by the fire.

"Don't feed that man!" ordered Jones, setting his horse up. "Don't give him a thing—unless he pays!"

"He's done paid," stated Sowbelly, regretfully.

"Well, don't feed him, anyhow! I don't want him around. Hereafter he's barred from the wagon!"

"You must think," observed Mace, "that I give a dam', anyway. I wouldn't eat your grub if I was starving. I just come by to see that false-alarm steer-roper of yourn. Does he still claim to be Champion of the World?"

"I sure do!" spoke up Tex McMullen. "And I've got the record to prove it."

"What record? What's your time? I'd just like to

match you for a contest! We'd soon find out who was best!"

"I win first money at Cheyenne, last July. Time twenty-two and four-fifths."

"*My* time was twenty-one seconds, flat!" boasted Mace. "And I'm the Champion of the World!"

"You are not, sir!" thundered the Colonel. "Both the steer and your horse fell down, the moment you crossed the line. That record does not count. You haven't equaled it, before or since!"

"I don't need to equal it," came back Long Rope, "to beat that big stiff of yours. I've got five thousand dollars in the Long Horn safe that says I can out-rope him, anytime. So put up or shut up—I reckon you'll shut up."

Breckenridge Jones sank back in his saddle and gasped, then straightened up and plucked at his goatee.

"You're nothing but an impostor!" he bawled. "How do I know that you've got any money? And if you mean this for a challenge at the next Rodeo, my men have been forbidden to compete!"

"That's good—that's fine!" said Mace. "It will give the local boys a chance. We showed you last spring, that we had the best hands, for roping or riding, either one. We made your Western Shows boys look like just what they are—a big bunch of show-offs, all silk shirts and calfskin vests. It's a good thing you quit, before we hoorawed you out of the country."

"Just a minute!" snapped Jones, beckoning his

champ to one side; and while they talked back and forth and Mace sat grinning, Sowbelly Johnson joined in.

"Have you got any money?" demanded the Colonel, looking up.

"Well—no!" responded Bowman. "Not here."

"But I understand," went on Jones, drawing closer. "I understand you just offered the cook a thousand dollar bill."

"Oh, that was last spring," jested Mace.

"No, right now!" repeated the Colonel. "If you'll put up that money I'll cover it."

"Yes! And who would hold the stakes? A man would be a sucker to put up his good money with a gang of robbers like you!"

"Aw, you're drunk!" scoffed Tex, reining away. "Always blowing about how much money you've got. You're a good skater all summer and a good swimmer all winter. But ump-umm—you won't put up a cent. How about that talk you've been making that you can rope ten steers to my one—each man to pick the other man's steers?"

"That goes!" answered Mace. "I'll match you, any time."

"For how much?" inquired the Colonel, wrathfully.

"For five thousand dollars and the Championship of the World."

"I'll take that bet," yapped Jones.

"All right," agreed Bowman, rising to go. "Put your money up with Cramer and he'll bet you five more.

But don't come crying around to the management if I happen to pick a bad steer."

"Heh! The same to you!" jeered Tex. "And ten of them!"

CHAPTER XXIII "HERE'S YOUR HAT!"

HOOKED, by grab!" laughed Long Rope as he rode away from the Hash-knife wagon. "I'll show 'em who's a good skater all summer, and a good talking-swimmer all winter. Wait till I get Tex McMullen into the arena with some steer that's too big for a box-car. That's when the yaller will come out!"

"Yes, but where are you going to get the steer?" asked Joe.

"Down in Mexico—down in Mexico—where they grow the real old long-horns! I've got him all staked out. This steer is so *bravo* he's killed three bullfighters and crippled a whole lot more. He's even killed grizzly bears. Ho-o-ly Smoke, but he's a bad one—and just think of old Tex, trying to snare him with that thirty-foot rope!"

He laughed again, raucously, and jumped Jug into a gallop.

"Got to get into town," he hollered back, "and tell Cramer about this bet."

"No you don't!" yelled Joe, dashing up. "You promised to go with me. I'm holding you to your word."

"Aw, listen!" reasoned Mace. "What's the use of going over there when both of us are in dead wrong? And you'll have to loosen up and do some real talking if you expect to make a winning with Eva."

"All right," agreed Joe. "But she's always making fun of me and saying how little I am. She says she's going to grow to be six feet tall, jest from drinking that limestone water!"

"Ha, ha! That's good!" laughed Long Rope. "And what did you say, then?"

"I didn't say nothing," sulked Joe.

"Well, you want to have a come-back," advised Mace, "if you expect to make a winning with Eva. You've got competition—men like Tex McMullen, that'll tell a poor young girl anything. But I'll go with you, Joe. Only remember this—our string is about played out. So talk up—play a leading hand!"

He reined Jug towards the east and they hit the trail at a gallop, in case the Colonel might be following behind; but as they neared the spring, and the big house on the hill, he pulled up and stared ahead.

"There she is!" he said, "doing stunts in the ring. Ain't she the cutest little thing that ever rode a horse? Look at that, now!" And Little Joe looked.

Standing upright on the back of her big white horse Little Eva was practicing her tricks. She jumped off and swung on again as with slow, measured strides the gentle circus horse loped down the track. Then, spinning out a loop, she leapt through it again and again, her yellow hair gleaming in the sun. In her silk tights and spreading skirts she looked like a butterfly, dancing and posing yet never wholly still; and Barfoot heaved a sigh.

"Let's stay here and watch her!" he proposed. But even as he spoke the huge, gorilla-like bouncer stepped out of his lodge and stood watching them. In the crystalline air they could see his bony skull and the long arms reaching to his knees, and when he spoke the fancy riding ceased. Half hidden behind the fence of her tan-bark ring Little Eva dropped down and out of sight and Joe rode ahead again, muttering.

"Doggone that blacksmith," he said. "Seems like he gits worse and worse. I ought to have pulled my six-shooter and warped him over the head with it the first time he opened his face."

"That's the talk!" encouraged Mace, "and it ain't too late yet. Go after him—I'll back your play."

"Nope—no rough stuff," vetoed Joe. "There's Merry Hart, out on the porch. I'm going to ride right up there—"

"And I'll stay behind," ended Long Rope.

"No, you come too," begged Barfoot. "And talk to her mother. Old Bluebeard will let us pass."

They clattered up to the gate, which swung open before them, but Bowman stopped to glare at the blacksmith.

"Any objections," he asked, "if we ride up to the big house and pay our respects to Miss Eva?"

"No, sir—none at all," returned Gilhooly; and Joe went straight ahead.

"If you have, just state 'em," invited Mace. But the Wild Irishman was obsequiousness itself.

"None whatever!" he replied, bowing lower than before; and then a strange thing happened.

As Brown Jug passed the gate and started up the hill Little Eva darted out from the horse-ring and ran along beside him.

"Hello, Túcumcari!" she said, smiling up at him, "I knew you'd come to see me!" Then, grabbing a saddle-string, she leapt lightly on behind and Jug bowed his head to buck.

"Oh—oh!" chuckled Mace, "he won't ride double!"

"Yes he will!" she shot back, tickling Brown Jug in the flanks; and when he crow-hopped they both laughed at once.

"You're getting so big and heavy he can't throw us!" jested Bowman as she grabbed him from behind and held on. "Never seen a girl grow like you have!"

"Do you think so?" she asked, anxiously. "I just hate being so small!"

"Oh, sure!" he said, "that's the first thing I noticed. Nothing like good hard grub and hard water to make a man grow tall!"

"Oh, glory!" she sighed, "I gained an inch last summer. But they all treat me like a child!"

"Well, ain't you a child?" he asked.

"Why, no," she cried, "I'm nearly eighteen!"

"Well, think of that!" he exclaimed, loosening her hands in a panic, "and me treating you so familiar, this way. You'd better get off or your mother will scold you!"

"Oh, no!" resisted Eva, "she'll scold me, anyhow. Let her talk to Joe for a minute—I want to ask you something!"

"Nope, nope!" answered Mace, still spurring up the hill, "that wouldn't be fair to Joe!"

"Yes, it would!" she pleaded. "It's something important!"

But he spurred inexorably on. She was Joe's girl, and this was Joe's day.

"I'll talk with your mother," he said.

"He gave me a ride!" crowed Little Eva, sliding gracefully down off of Jug. "Good morning, Mr. Barfoot!"

"Good morning!" returned Joe, brightening up, but Merry Hart never smiled.

"Did you see Colonel Jones?" she asked as she ushered them into the house; and right there the pardners' teamwork broke down.

"Sure!" responded Bowman bluntly; but Joe shook his head and said: "No."

"Oh, did you have some trouble?" she demanded anxiously; and Joe turned scowling as Mace spoke.

"Oh, no!" he replied. "No trouble at all—did we, Joe? But I did have some words with that show-off, Tex McMullen."

"And what did *he* say?" inquired Eva mischievously.

"Well," began Long Rope, "we were talking about steer-tying and a brag that I made one time. And he said I was one of these kind that's a good swimmer all winter and a good skater all summer. I reckon you know what that means?"

"Oh, yes," returned Little Eva. "And what did *you* say, then?"

"I told the swelled-up toad I was a better man than he was, any time. Then I offered to bet him I could tie down ten steers while he was tying one, and the poor fool took me up. Or that is, your father did—for five thousand dollars, at the next Rodeo."

"Oh, Mother, can't I stay to see it?" pleaded Eva. "I'll do whatever you say!"

"No, dear," answered Merry Hart firmly. "I don't think it's best." And Little Eva burst into tears.

"What's the matter?" blurted out Joe as they sat in stunned silence. "Is Miss Eva going away?"

"She is going East to school," announced her mother, "to complete her education."

"Well, can't I come *back,* then?" begged Eva, looking up. "I've just *got* to see that match!"

"No, now Eva," soothed Merry Hart, "you know how your father feels. And how *I* feel, too. It's time you quit your lawless ways and learned to be a lady."

"Who, Eva?" spoke up Mace, taking the defensive. "A queen couldn't act any nicer. And what can they learn her, back there? She's the finest rider in the country, already!"

"Yes, but you don't understand, Mr. Bowman, how lawless and defiant she has become. She went into town only day before yesterday and testified against her father in that suit!"

"Why, Mother!" protested Eva, "I never was so surprised in my life as when that funny Mr. Cramer called my name. I had just slipped in and sat down. But when he asked me, straight out, if I thought Mr. Bowman would steal—"

"That will do!" broke in her mother, severely. "Now you and Mr. Barfoot go out on the porch. I'd like a few words with Mr. Bowman. And if you see your father coming, let me know."

She drew her mouth down grimly as she watched them out the door and as he saw the steely look in her eyes Mace Bowman caught his breath. They were like the eyes of a gunfighter, cold and devoid of all fear, and when she turned them on him he flinched. But now as by a miracle they were suddenly soft and womanly, and a sweet smile parted her lips.

"You're not a bad man, Mr. Bowman," she said. "May I ask you to do me a favor?"

"Why, sure!" he answered heartily.

"Please don't come to see my daughter any more. It just puts silly ideas into her head and makes her hard to manage. And please don't write her any letters."

"Who—me? I never write to anybody!"

"Yes, I know," she said, "but she's going away."

"Well, all right," he replied, "then I couldn't see her, anyway. And if I'd known, Mrs. Jones, that I wasn't welcome I'd never have come through your gates."

He rose up angrily but she motioned him back.

"Don't misunderstand me," she said. "As far as I'm

concerned you are perfectly welcome, but I have to consider my husband."

"Well, one is about as friendly as the other," he responded, "your husband, the blacksmith, or you. 'Here's your hat—don't hurry,' is the best I get from any of you. I'll bid you good-by, Mrs. Jones."

"Good-by," she smiled graciously. "And thank you, Mr. Bowman."

"Oh, don't mention it," he answered scathingly, and strode out talking to himself.

Little Eva and Joe were standing on the porch and he passed them without a glance. But as he swung up on his horse Eva took a run and landed expertly behind him.

"Where are you going?" she demanded as Brown Jug began to buck. "Oh, hold me—I'm falling off!"

With a downhill slant Jug was doing more than crowhop—he was pitching, and Mace reached back one hand. Then as he found her inside his arm he held her tight and let Brown Jug do his worst. They bucked off down the road and, hearing the tumult, Gilhooly came rushing forth.

"Don't drop me!" she begged as she felt his grip loosen; and Bowman laughed as the blacksmith barred his way.

"I'm stealing her!" he hollered. "Look out or I'll run over you!" And Little Eva laughed and clung closer.

"I only wish you were!" she sighed as they dashed out into the open.

"Nope," he said, "your mother made me promise I'd never come to see you again."

"Well, good-by, then!" she panted, kicking Jug to make him pitch; and in the tumult of his bucking she kissed Mace on the cheek and vaulted to the ground. "Good-by!" she called after him, waving her hand and smiling wistfully. "I'll be back, Túcumcari! Whoopeelah!"

CHAPTER XXIV *MY* GIRL!

FREE at last of his double load and outraged at his treatment, Brown Jug broke his pitching-spell and took the trail at a gallop while his master gave him the reins. He was almost as much astonished as Brown Jug himself at this avalanche of silken tights and fluffy skirts that had descended upon him as he fled. How her slender arms had clung to him as they had bucked down the hill and out on the open plain! And when he had started to drop her she had kicked Jug in the flanks and started him bucking again. Then, right in the midst of it, he had felt her breath against his cheek and Little Eva had kissed him!

With the best of intentions Mace had tried to remember that Eva was Little Joe's girl. But now he knew better—she was his! Neither the blacksmith, the Colonel nor Merry Hart had been able to keep them apart. Little Joe was out of luck, that was all.

He came whipping up behind, taking his rage out

on Punkin until he could catch up with Bowman.

"You're a fine pardner!" he railed. "What are you trying to do—steal my girl?"

"I'm trying to get away, before Merry Hart kills me. She's the Champion Rifle-shot of the World and she told me pintedly to git!"

"She did not!" came back Barfoot. "I heard every word of it. Eva and I were listening through the door."

"Well, did it sound like I was trying to steal your girl, then, you complaining little shrimp? What are you all bowed up about, now?"

"You grabbed her away from me the minute you came out and took her down the hill! And I seen you, dadram it—you kissed her!"

"I did not! Jug was pitching, and she grabbed me!"

"Yes, and you grabbed her! A trick and fancy rider! Was you afraid she might fall off?"

"Oh, well, she was just joking, I reckon. She says: 'Look out—I'm falling off!' But what's the difference? She'll never be back."

"W'y, you doggoned liar!" yelled Little Joe. "The last thing she said was, she *would* be."

Mace reined in abruptly and looked Little Joe over.

"Say," he said, "you're getting hard to suit. I just came along to get you past that blacksmith and now you're on the warpath. I reckon right here is where we split the blankets. You can get some other guy to cuss."

"Suits me," assented Barfoot bitterly, "you're no pardner of mine. And you keep away from my girl."

"Your girl, nothing!" retorted Mace. "You never had no girl. And you never will have till you learn to whip your own blacksmiths. Take a club if you can't use your hands."

"I don't need any advice from *you!*" snapped Joe. "There's the road—which way will you go?"

"Right back to El Toro, where I was going in the first place. Which way are you traveling, Mr. Barfoot?"

"Wherever they take Eva I'm going to follow her," answered Joe; and Long Rope gazed at him scornfully.

"Yes, and show what a dam' fool you are," he said. "Come on, Jug!" And he jabbed him with the spurs.

Long Rope was mad, but not as mad as he seemed, and as he galloped off towards town he forgot all about Joe and the rest of them. For had not Little Eva hugged him and given him a kiss, right in the middle of Brown Jug's bucking fit? And where in all the West was there another girl like that—half as pretty, half as gay, half as quick to step up on a horse? He slapped Jug and laughed as he took the long trail. She was *his* girl, and had been from the first.

Joe had made his big mistake when he had hollered for help instead of taking care of Gilhooly himself. She had kissed Little Joe to make good her word, but the true "reward" had gone to the battler. How she had laughed when he took old Bluebeard's anvil and threw it down the bottomless spring! And ever since that time she had scorned Joe Barfoot and gone out of her way to meet *him.*

With all the world to choose from she had taken a fancy to the fighting cowboy from Túcumcari, and he had lost his heart the first day. But Joe Barfoot had stood between them, with his preposterous ideas of courting and his claim that he had seen Eva first; and now, when she had kissed Mace and laid her heart at his feet, it was too late even to go back. Merry Hart had exacted his promise not to write to Eva or see her —and the Bowmans kept their word. But perhaps she would come to him!

Getting the best of scheming mothers and over-bearing stepfathers was rather a gift with Eva. Even when, as on that day, Merry Hart had worked fast, Little Eva had listened in and worked faster. Just as he came running out and jumped up on his horse to get away from it all, she had grabbed at a saddle-string and vaulted up behind him, killing all his anger with one laugh. Then she had pretended to fall off—to be carried away by her gallant knight—and at last, as they parted, she had kissed him! Well, Cramer had been right—a woman's heart was her own. If he never saw her again, he would know she had forgotten him. And if she loved him, Eva would come back!

The genial barkeeper was watching for him when he stepped into the Long Horn and, crooking one finger, he beckoned him in behind and rang the bell for the drinks.

"That five thousand dollars has been covered," he said. "Now what's the next thing to do?"

"Go down to Chihuahua City and buy that fighting

stag, before the Hash-knives get hold of him. But we don't need to worry about that. A cheap screw like Colonel Jones will never spend a thousand for one stag when the mountains are full of wild steers. Ten to one odds is enough for him, and the Rodeo doesn't come off till next spring. So, just to keep him guessing, I'll drop out of sight. But when I come back—hold your breath!"

"You'll have that big steer with you, eh?"

"The size of a mountain!" nodded Mace. "And fierce as a grizzly bear! There ain't but one horse in the Hash-knife string that would even pretend to stand up to him—and that horse is Scrambled Eggs!"

"What do you mean?" inquired Cramer as Mace smiled, knowingly.

"I mean," said Long Rope, "I'm going to get that horse. And I'm not going to steal him, either. Did you ever think, Cramer, that that Hash-knife brand could be improved? Now here, lemme show you what I mean."

He drew on a piece of paper the well-known Hash-knife iron and began to make his alterations.

"Up over the top," he said, "we'll burn in big letters: MEALS. And underneath: 25 CENTS!"

"Very interesting, I'm sure," observed Cramer. "But what is the big idea?"

"The Colonel," expounded Mace, "will never enter a horse with 'Meals Twenty-five Cents' on his hip. They'd laugh him out of the stands. He'll sell that horse, Cramer, and ship him out of the country to keep it from being known. But I'll trace him and buy him back. Then, when them wild steers are fighting their heads and Brown Jug is all played out, I'll step into the corral and come out on Scrambled Eggs! Do you reckon that'll get a laugh?"

"It'll bring down the house!" predicted Cramer admiringly. "You've got quite a brain, Brother Bowman."

"Yes, and that ain't all," boasted Long Rope. "I'm going to catch Whistling Rufus!"

"Aha!" exclaimed the barkeep. "But still—I don't know. Every horse-catcher in this country has made a try for him—"

"Except me!" broke in Bowman. "I'll get him. They've had too many people on these horse-drives. I figure on working alone."

"That would be a great feat," stated Cramer. "But how do you expect to do it?"

"Don't ask me to *tell* you," answered Long Rope airily. "I'm from Túcumcari, savvy, where all the mustangers come from! I'll bring him in for the big Rodeo!"

He started for the door, but the barkeeper stopped him.

"How did you come out with Eva?" he asked.

"Fine!" replied Mace. "She kissed me good-by. But me and Joe have split up."

"I see," nodded Cramer. "Is she going away?"

"Back East—and I promised not to write to her."

"Hmm," observed the barkeeper. "Her mother, eh? Well, what shall I say if Miss Eva should inquire for you? Any word you'd like to leave?"

"You tell her," said Mace, "I'll never forget that kiss. And the next time she kisses me like that I'm going to run away with her. Can you remember all that, Mr. Cramer?"

"Word for word," responded Cramer, soberly; and as Bowman danced out he sighed.

CHAPTER XXV THE RAWHIDE

EL Toro woke up to find Long Rope gone, and no one could find even his horse-tracks, but far out across the desert towards Whisky Lake a lone wisp of dust touched the sky. For great words demand great deeds, and he had said he would catch Whistling Rufus. Other mustangers had tried and failed, but Mace had Little Elsie for his aide.

She followed along willingly at the end of a stout rope that was tied to a Mexican hackamore, for all the months that she had been penned up the canyon she had spent looking over the gate. Perhaps, in the night, her lord Whistling Rufus had ventured near in search of his *manada;* or perhaps the desert wind, blowing in from Whisky Lake, had brought his scent to LC. But she knew he was there and that night in their hidden camp she snorted and snuffed the breeze.

Whisky Lake was a great flat, miles across, with a water-hole out in the middle pawed deep by wild horses and burros. Around its rim, a dense growth of mesquite trees marked the margin of the waters during floods; and, concealed in their midst, Bowman had found the high corral which the horse-catchers had built for a trap. It was set on the edge of a little opening among the trees, but he made his camp far away.

Little Elsie fretted and stamped and fought against her rope, while from across the wide flat there came the braying of burros as they trooped out to drink at the water-hole. Feed was short on the great desert that extended for miles and miles to the banks of the Rio Grande, and the water was shorter yet. A drouth was on the land and the cattle had drifted back to the high, cool canyons of the Guadalupes. But as Little Elsie stood, head up and ears erect, listening to every sound of the night; from far out in the sandhills there came a whistling snort and she answered, loud and shrill. It was Whistling Rufus, coming in!

Bowman heard the stamp of his hoofs as he circled around the camp where he could catch the taint on the wind; and then, whistling angrily, the stud scampered away, only to come back and snuff again. But his fears had made him wary and, after a drink at the lake, he drifted off into the night. Little Elsie neighed and whinnied as she sensed his retreat, each call trailing off into a choking sob that ended with a plunge against her rope. But Rufus had learned his lesson in the horse-trap at Cedar Spring and at dawn he was nowhere to be seen.

Mace penned the mare in the stout corral and rode out to pick up his trail; and at last, far ahead in the sandhills, he saw the great stallion watching him. He stood on the summit of a mound of drifted sand—his long mane whipping the wind, his tail raised like a flag—all set to quit the country on the run. Bowman halted on a dune and looked him over through his glasses before he turned away. The stud was seal-fat, though the desert was bare of grass; and that could only come from eating the mesquite-beans that grew around Whisky Lake. As high as they could reach the short-necked burros had plucked them off, but Rufus could feed far above them. He would never leave the lake.

Circling off to the north to conceal his return, Bowman scouted along the lake-shore until he was satisfied that Rufus lived there. Then, afire to have his trap set, he loped back to the corral and worked all day at the gate. It was a huge one, hung downhill so it would close of itself, and until almost dark Mace rigged springs and strung trigger-ropes to release it at a touch. Little Elsie watched him anxiously, stamping her feet as she strained against her rope; and when all was set Bowman put her inside and rode out into the night.

Dragging his pack animal behind him and mounted on Brown Jug he took the backtrail towards town. Then, far out on the desert, he made a dry camp and waited for the dawn. But when he rode back his trap was still set, though Whistling Rufus's tracks were everywhere. He had come up to the gate, but even in the darkness he had sensed the hidden ropes. Not once had he overstepped the line where they lay half-buried in the sand.

Bowman strung his ropes again and took himself away, but neither time nor art could dull the fierce distrust of this stud who had been trapped and had escaped. For two days and nights, without coming back, Mace left Elsie tied in the corral; but when he returned he found his tricks set at naught—Whistling Rufus had not entered the gate. He knew it was a trap, and Little Elsie with all her coaxing could never make him forget.

All day through his glasses Bowman watched for the stallion while he racked his brains for new schemes. Whistling Rufus was educated to every trick and device that was known to the mustanger's craft. He knew traps and snares and swinging gates—there was nothing left but the chase. But to run Rufus down on this limitless plain, how many relay riders and fresh strings of mounts would be necessary to insure success! He was fat and strong and tireless as the wind. Only Little Elsie could keep up with his fast pace, and Elsie was still a bronk. She had submitted to being led at the strong bite of the hackamore—but could he break her of that swift, circling buck?

At dusk the wary stallion trotted out on the dry lake and challenged the horse-hunter's fire. He was angry now because Bowman had returned, and exploded in deep-lunged snorts. And Elsie, eager to join him, made the night hideous with her nickering until Long Rope was completely worn out.

"What's the matter with you?" he yelled, rising up at dawn and stamping on his boots. "I'll tame you, you old rip, and Whistling Rufus, to boot. I don't *need* to break you to ride!"

He grabbed up an old cowhide that had been left at his camp and rattled it in her face, and Little Elsie flew back.

"Well!" he said, "you don't like it, eh? Just wait till I cut a hole in the middle and I'll ram it plumb over your head. Then you can chase Rufus and Rufus can lead the way, and we'll see who gives out first."

He snatched up an ax and hacked a hole in the hide, while Little Elsie snorted and backed; but at a far call from Rufus she raised her head again and gave an answering neigh.

"I'll fix you," he muttered, working away with enthusiasm as the new idea grew upon him. He fashioned the hole to fit her neck, snapped a loop over her forefeet and laid her on her side with a jerk. Then he rammed the stiff rawhide over her head, untied her and set her free.

"Now—run!" he said and, wearing the hide like a ruff, Little Elsie dashed off across the lake-bed. In the distance, still whistling, Rufus stood against the sky; but as Elsie clattered towards him he exploded in mighty snorts and plunged out of sight to escape. Bowman stepped up on Jug and went galloping after them, stopping on each high hill to look; and always Whistling Rufus was fleeing on ahead and Elsie followed close in his wake.

They were well-matched for this race across sandhills and plains, the stallion as free and tireless as the wind itself and the old mare rejoicing in her freedom. But though she strained every nerve to catch up with her mate, the flapping ruff of cowhide stampeded him afresh every time that he stopped and looked back. From the summit of a knoll Bowman watched them through his glasses until they became a line of dust on the horizon; and then, true to their instincts, they circled and turned back and Long Rope shook out a loop.

Here was a new way of catching horses, with the mare doing the chasing and the mustanger waiting at the start; but when Rufus came galloping back he crossed the dry lake like a streak and Bowman let him go. Why should he jerk down his horse and put up a battle against Rufus when, still eager to join her mate, Little Elsie was hot on his trail? Let the race go on for days and days, as long as he could see their dust. And, when the flight ended, there, worn-out and leg-weary, Whistling Rufus would be waiting for the rope.

All that day, with short pauses, the restless horses fled on; one animated by a fear of the rattling hide, the other drawn on by her love. Bowman watched them with awe and the growing conviction that in the morning even their dust would be lost; but at dawn he picked it up, far out in the sandhills, and once more they came doubling back. They went chasing across the lake-bed like lost souls out of purgatory, doomed to flee on forever before the winds of evil chance – one pursuing, the other leading on. But no matter how far they ran Rufus always came circling back, and at last Mace saw his pace slacken.

It was late in the afternoon when from the circle of mesquite trees Brown Jug, fresh and eager, made his charge; and before Whistling Rufus could summon his failing strength a rope settled over his head. Bowman snaked him, spent and blown, inside the high corral; and there at last Little Elsie, relieved of her cowhide, was able to join her liege lord. Long Rope slammed the heavy gate and bound it fast with rawhide thongs, then he looked down on Rufus and laughed.

CHAPTER XXVI IN THE BREAKING PEN

WHISTLING Rufus was caught, but his fighting spirit was untamed, and when at dawn Long Rope peered over the gate he hurled himself against the fence. Then he rose up, shaking his head, and turned to face his captor; but Bowman had dropped out of sight. The stallion had recovered his strength, and not till the sun was hot did Mace come back to the corral. But now he bore a bucket of water for a peace-offering, and Little Elsie forgot she was wild.

For three days and two nights, with a cowhide around her neck, she had raced across the desert sands. Her flanks were drawn in, her haggard eyes bloodshot and she trotted up to beg for a drink. But at the back of the corral, still hampered by the drag-rope which had been hung around his neck, Whistling

Rufus stood sullenly, his arched neck held low, every breath a snort of defiance. Bowman took away the bucket and lashed the gate fast and the next morning he tried again.

The stallion sucked his lips as he heard the slosh of water and saw his mate go to drink. For a moment he forgot his deep-seated enmity, for his flanks were gaunted terribly; but after the first step forward he drew back snorting and Mace closed the gate and went out. He returned with a big armful of mesquite-tops which he threw down for Elsie to eat, then all through the heat of the day he left the big stud to think.

He was not a vicious horse, old Whistling Rufus, but even after four days of famine and thirst he remembered his hatred of mankind. He was weak now, starved down until his eyes were glazed and sunken, and he advanced halfway to the gate; but he would not come and drink and inexorably Long Rope left him, to fret through the long, parching night. There was in the stallion such an excess of vital energy that even at dawn he could snort, but at the smell of the water he forgot his ancient grudge and charged in to claim his drink.

With an angry squeal he shouldered Elsie aside, snapping his teeth to drive her back; and then with a sigh he thrust his head into the bucket and drank up every drop. After that he was cured of his fear of this lone man who came and went so quietly. When Bowman returned with a huge armful of mesquite-tops he drove Elsie off again. He stripped the leaves from the thorny twigs to kill the first, fierce pangs of his hunger; and then there came another surprise.

Mounted on sturdy Brown Jug, Mace rode into the corral and shook out his long, snaky loop. Rufus circled the pen, snorting, all his old fears renewed; but when he wheeled and made a charge to leap at the high fence Bowman roped him by his two front-feet. There was a jerk on the saddle-horn, a grunt and a thump and the stallion lay sprawling in the dust. That first terrific fall took all the fight out of him and before he could rise Mace was kneeling on his neck, adjusting the rough rawhide hackamore.

At the end of the taut throw-rope Brown Jug stood like a statue, holding the two front-feet from the ground, and after the breaking-halter was on Bowman picked up the drag-rope that had been left on Rufus from the first. It was a two-inch well-rope, strong enough to hold anything, and with a deft flip of the slack Mace noosed one hind-foot and drew it up toward his neck. Then he manacled the two front-feet with a pair of rawhide hobbles and turned Whistling Rufus loose.

He reared up, struggling and fighting the hobbles, and the well-rope that held his hind-foot; and after watching him a while Bowman threw open the gate and let Brown Jug and Elsie out. Now if ever the wild stud could be conquered, while his strength was at its lowest ebb; but first he let him fight and kick against the ropes that held him like iron bands. He fell back, he rolled over, he lay grunting on his side, until at last he stretched out panting, too tired to open his eyes.

Bowman walked up, speaking gently, knelt down to pat his neck, to loosen the biting ropes; but Rufus made no sign. He was worn out, starved and beaten; all his great strength had fled and so he submitted to his fate. Mace unlashed the well-rope and threw his hind-foot loose and still he lay puffing in the dust, but when the cowboy stepped away and pulled at the hackamore he scrambled to his feet with a jerk. The braided circle of the *bosal* had pressed down on his tender nostrils, cutting off his breath at one touch.

Whistling Rufus stared intently at the two-legged creature that stood holding the slender rope. Then with a fierce, impatient leap he headed for the fence and the breaking-halter fetched him up short. As long as he stood still, the heavy circlet of rawhide hung suspended by the cheek-straps; but at the least resisting pull the cunningly rigged halter drew down and choked off his breath. He set back stubbornly, shaking his head like a hooked trout, thrashing and struggling until he landed in the dirt; and as he gave up and quit fighting the smothering *bosal* was released and he sucked in a great gasp of air.

Once more the man spoke to him, and as he slackened the rope Rufus rose up tottering on his feet. He was weak, too weak to snort and fly hack against the rope which he knew would cut off his breath, and when Bowman tugged gently he took a step forward to avoid its ruthless grip. Bowman pulled again and Rufus stepped again until at last he had learned to lead. Then Mace went out and, fetching a big bucket of water, led him up to drink.

The next day, when he came back, Whistling Rufus had forgotten his lesson. He was snorty and evil-eyed and at the first pull on his tender nose he flung himself against the hackamore in a frenzy. But Bowman sat back grimly on the end of the rope, digging his high heels into the ground, and when the dust cleared away Rufus was sitting back on his haunches with his eyes bulging out of his head. But he had learned all over again not to resist the biting rope, learned to respond to the slightest pull, and the cowboy fed him again. But only enough to keep him alive, for the great battle was yet to come.

At the end of four days Rufus had forgotten his first fear and when his master came striding in with water from the hole he whinnied as he heard his steps. Not once since his long race had his great thirst been fully quenched, and hunger still kept his flanks gaunt; but when Bowman tied him down and cinched his saddle on his back, Whistling Rufus had wall-eyed fits. He kicked, he bucked, he dashed against the fence when he found himself up and free; but at the end of it all the saddle was still there and the fighting had sapped his strength.

Long Rope worked with him day by day, trying to conquer his panicky fear without breaking his fighting heart; until at last, swinging up into the saddle, he sat waiting for the final battle to begin. Rufus looked back startled when, as the blind was pulled up, he saw a man on his back. Then he bowed his stubborn head and leapt straight at the moon while Bowman gave him the spurs. At the first jab in his flank the stallion kicked like a flash, almost knocking Mace's boot from the stirrup.

The rowel rang like a bell before it hooked him in the neck, and Rufus began to bawl. Then he settled down to hard, steady bucking until the cowboy's head snapped back. He jumped and whirled about in mid-air, bawling and snapping his white teeth as he landed with a devastating jar, but to fall off beneath those feet was to court instant death and Long Rope clamped his knees and rode. He was holding to the horn and there was blood on his shirt-front when the stallion stopped dead in his tracks. Every muscle in his tense shoulders was quivering from weariness, his feet spread, and he sank to carth, beaten.

Bowman slid off weakly and sat down on Rufus's neck while he waited for the world to come straight. Then he staggered to the gate and gave himself a big drink out of the bucket he carried for the horse. He was leaning against the fence while his strength came back and his vital organs shifted into place when there was a snort from within—a low, pleading nicker—and Whistling Rufus rattled the gate.

"All right, Rufe," responded Long Rope and, struggling to his feet, he gave his new pet a drink.

CHAPTER XXVII
MATADOR—THE MAN-KILLER

It had been a fight to the finish and Bowman had won, but after a big drink from the bucket Whistling Rufus showed no resentment. Mace fed him and petted him, lugging oil cans of water to slake his ten-day thirst; and the next time he swung up into the saddle the stallion only crow-hopped and stopped. It was the fear in his heart which had put him on the warpath, and now that he found that the man was his friend he just bucked enough to be sociable. At the end of a week Long Rope was out in the open, chasing burros and roping off his back.

Day by day Bowman lingered at the lonely lake, cutting down his rations to bait Whistling Rufus while he taught him to rein and rope. Then at last, traveling by night, he took his prize back to Hockaday's and they put him behind the high gate. The fighting stallion stood still as his saddle and bridle were stripped off and Mace gave him a slap on the neck.

"Go on, now," he said; but Rufus turned back and nuzzled at his pocket.

"By grab, boys!" spoke up Hockaday, "he's gentle as a dog." But Bowman shook his head.

"Don't you think it," he said. "He'll kick, strike and bite the first time ary one of you comes near. He's a one-man horse and you want to keep away from him. But with me he's a regular old sugar-bum."

He reached into his pocket and fetched out the biscuit which Rufus had been demanding, and still he did not go. From the depths of Black Canyon mysterious figures appeared and Elsie nickered vehemently, but Whistling Rufus only snorted. They were the mares and colts of his lost *manada,* but for the moment even his horse-band seemed strange.

"Get out of here!" laughed Bowman, giving him a last, friendly slap; and with a high, whistling leap he was gone.

"That's Rufus!" observed Hockaday with a sigh. "How much do you want for him, Mace?"

"You keep him," suggested Long Rope, "and give me every other colt. Keep him plumb out of sight until after the Rodeo. I might need him if Jug should get hurt."

"Listen heah, boy!" warned Uncle Ben, "don't you put him in the ring agin any of them longhorned steers. That's the finest breeding-stallion in New Mexico. I'll fix you up fur rope-hawses, as many as you need, but Rufus is too good to git gored."

"Well, then listen," confided Mace, "I've got a scheme of my own for getting some A-1 mounts—Hash-knife horses that might be used against me. Do you remember Scrambled Eggs? Well, now maybe—mind you, maybe—something might happen to Eggs; and I'm going to be out of the country. Down in Chihuahua, buying bad steers. But if anything *should* happen and they'd ship him out of the country, you buy him for me—understand?"

"As much as I need to, I reckon," grunted Hockaday. "All right, I'll keep my eye on him."

"Send a puncher over that way in about a week," suggested Bowman, "and have him scout around. And when you do find Eggs bring him back here at night and keep him hid up the canyon. We've got to stand together, Uncle Ben, if we're going to improve North America!"

"She shore needs improving," observed Hockaday, ambiguously; and Mace rode away into the night. Three days later, in the midst of a blinding sandstorm, he appeared just at sundown in the lower Hash-knife pasture and put a rope on the startled Scrambled Eggs. Then in the bottom of a deep wash he heated a saddle-ring and made some improvements on his brand. It was a dirty trick to play on the game little horse, and Mace apologized when he turned him loose.

"Never mind, Pet," he said, "it won't be long now until you're working for a real Champeen!"

Then he spurred Brown Jug south into the teeth of the wind, and when next heard of in New Mexico it was spring. Spring, with the grass standing high on the plains and Pioneer Day just starting. There were bill-boards in three States announcing the Contest of the Century to decide the Championship of the World: Tex McMullen vs. Long Rope Bowman, for a purse of $5000!

But that was just the purse. There was ten thousand

dollars more in the Long Horn safe that went to the man who won. And thousands of dollars on the side. El Toro was in a turmoil as the long-expected stock-car came rumbling in on the freight and was shunted out to the Park; and on the top of it, waving his hat, stood Mace Bowman himself, though it had been confidently stated he had skipped. Half the turmoil on the streets was between Hash-knife adherents and the friends of the redoubtable Túcumcari, for after all their boasting the Hash-knife boys woke up to find themselves called at last.

In a specially built corral at the Park they had penned the ten wildest steers in New Mexico. Their horns curved and curved again until they stretched six feet across, and their shoulders were humped with the weight. One hundred dollars apiece had been offered at the round-ups; and, not to leave anything to chance, Colonel Jones had sent off for more. They were the fiercest aggregation of stags and steers that had ever been assembled in the West.

But when Long Rope came riding in on top of his stock-car, from which there came a thumping of horns, every cowboy in town made a break for the Park to listen to that sinister sound. The car was locked and sealed, but from the Stygian darkness within there came a bawl that made their blood run cold. A bawl and a throaty rumble, and the door bulging from its moorings as Matador made a charge.

"That's him, boys!" announced Bowman, cheerily, "the biggest steer on earth. The man that ties to him will know he's been working before old Matador is throwed. Hello, Red! Howdy, Phat! Did you get all my money down? He's the Champeen Man-killer of Chihuahua!"

There was a deeper, throatier bawl, a high *mmm-woo-woo* as the monster complained against his fate; then the door rattled and jumped before the impact of his weight and a silence fell on the crowd.

"How many people has he killed?" shrilled a boy.

"Three bullfighters in one month," answered Long Rope promptly, "before he was barred from the ring. I wouldn't tie to him for the whole Hash-knife outfit. Listen to that, now!" And Matador charged again.

"Lawd A'mighty!" exclaimed Ben Hockaday, admiringly. "Who wants to bet on Tex?"

There was another tense silence, then a loud, derisive whoop and the crowd made a break for town. But not a dollar of Hash-knife money was to be found on the streets, for the news of the man-killer had spread. Back at the car, one favored friend after the other peered in through the high, barred window and as the huge, towering form of Matador filled their eyes they dropped down and sped away. Mace kept his perch, laughing, and as the crowd thinned out he saw Little Joe riding up. But it was not the same Joe with whom he had parted in anger, for now he was all a-grin.

"Hello, Mace!" he hailed. "Say, if I bring down my girl will you let her look at that steer?"

"Who—Eva?" answered Bowman. And his heart gave a great leap and stopped.

"Naw—Winnie! Winnie Bergman!" came back Joe. "I quit Eva, long ago."

"That so?" observed Mace as Joe climbed nimbly up and stared down into the gloom. "What's the matter—wasn't she good enough for you?"

"Oh, Eva was all right," returned Little Joe, absently, "but—my Gawd, is that all one steer?"

"The one and only," nodded Long Rope. "But say, who's Winnie Bergman?"

"The finest little girl in the world!" boasted Joe. "They's nothing high and mighty about her. She don't stand on no box so she can pat you on the head and ask you how come you don't grow!"

"When was this?" inquired Bowman, laughing. "Did you follow Eva clear back East?"

"Hell—no!" exclaimed Joe in disgust. "I went right back to Bottomless Spring."

"What? The same day Merry Hart run us off?"

"You bet your boots!" replied Barfoot. "I don't let no Champion Rifle-shot stand between me and seeing my girl. But I made a mistake, Mace, and I might as well apologize; because we hadn't been talking five minutes before Eva done patted me on the haid!"

"W'y, the little mischief!" grinned Bowman. "How tall is this Winnie girl, Joe?"

"She comes up to my chin, and she's twenty-two years old. We're going to git married right soon!"

"Good!" approved Mace. "You're showing some sense, now. What happened to Little Eva?"

"She went back East and that's the last I ever heard

of her. You wait till I bring Winnie over. She's the prettiest little girl—and part Indian, like me. The Bergmans are old-timers in this country."

"Fine!" nodded Long Rope. "I'll be glad to meet the lady and tell her what a good husband you'll make. Going in on the steer-tying, this year?"

"Nope—too dangerous!" replied Little Joe. "Winnie's afraid that something might happen to me."

"Well, what about the calf-tying, then?"

"She's afraid my horse might fall down."

"I—see!" responded Mace. "She must love you, Joe. Nobody cares whether I get busted or not."

"You bet ye she loves me!" affirmed Barfoot. "But don't you never hear from Eva?"

"Not a word," answered Long Rope truthfully. "The Old Lady warned me off."

"Aw—*her!*" scoffed Joe. "Don't let that stand in your way. Look at me and how I won Winnie. Go in and win—don't take 'No' for an answer! Just have a little nerve, like me!"

"Well, Joe," said Mace, "I believe maybe you're right. Only I reckon I'd better wait until I've tied them ten steers. My horse might slip and fall."

"Well—maybe," conceded Joe. "But say, there's Winnie!" And he rode off on the lope.

CHAPTER XXVIII "I PASS!"

THE Steer-Roping Contest between Mace Bowman and Tex McMullen had been heralded far and wide and on the morning of the great day the excursion trains pulled in until El Toro was swamped with guests. They came from as far as El Paso and Santa Fe, with sports from all over the West, but the rank and file were cattlemen from every ranch within a hundred miles. It was a battle for supremacy, with no quarter asked or given, a gladiatorial contest and bull-fight combined, the wildest Rodeo in the West.

To draw the crowd for the Pioneer Day Contests it had been scheduled for the day before, and when Neil Monroe and Cramer beheld the people flocking in they greeted their fellow-merchants with broad smiles. Thousands of dollars had been spent in exploiting this contest between the two pretenders for the crown, and it was heralded as a grudge fight between them, each trying to get the other man killed. Each contender had scoured the country for the wildest steers, to tax his opponent's skill; and if, in the contest, either one quit or weakened the title was to pass by default.

But it was more than a match between two chance men who had broken all records in the past. It was a contest between a cowboy, fresh from the range, and a professional roper from a show. Mace Bowman wore a jumper such as the mountain-boys used as a protection against brush and sharp horns; but Tex McMullen, even for this desperate test, clung to the silk shirt and gaudy rigging of a show-hand. He kept his rope short, after the custom of his kind, the quicker to bust his steer; but Túcumcari rode out with a fifty-foot whale-line, and a spare rope on the back of his saddle.

To fend off the wild steers from the crowded stands a woven wire fence had been built around the arena, every post set deep in the ground. A special corral had been erected to hold the Hash-knife steers, but in the high log pen that had been assigned to Mace he kept only his rope horses, under guard. The big cattle-car which held Matador was spotted at the chutes ready to open, and so with all set and the grandstands full, the signal was given to start.

Tex McMullen rode in first on the big, Roman-nosed black that he had selected to do battle with Matador; and as he trotted down the track Colonel Jones from his box rose up and led the cheers. Tex bowed right and left, sitting easily in his saddle, glancing about with a confident smile. But when Long Rope appeared he looked straight ahead, grimly, for he was to open the bout. Brown Jug arched his neck and jogged along steadily until they passed in through the gate; and then, up at the chutes, they turned out a huge steer—the roughest old moss-horn in the bunch.

He came out on the trot, head up and tail flying, swinging his feet to the front like piston rods; but when he crossed the line Brown Jug dashed in after him and Long Rope rose for the throw. They had passed the middle of the arena when the great loop shot forward and settled down over both horns—for that was the rule of the contest, that the animal must be roped by the neck. Fore-footing was barred, but after the steer was caught he could be busted in any way whatever.

Bowman whirled a wide loop, to encircle the spreading horns, and jerked it taut as it struck; but the steer got one foot through the noose and the Hashknife boys gave a whoop. Their steers were so big, their horns so wide, that here at the first throw Mace had got into a tangle and the animal was turning to fight. He hooked back at Brown Jug with a loud, defiant blat, his horn swooping low as he charged; but the slack of the rope tripped him up and when he rose Mace was right on his tail. With the bight of his rope he lashed him over the rump, and then they lined out in a chase.

Round and round the big arena they went at a gallop, the steer dragging the rope, the horse trying to get by him and the rider eating the dust. Then in a jamb the steer stopped and turned back towards the corral and Brown Jug galloped past him. They had slowed him down at last and, as Long Rope threw his slack to the right, Brown Jug hit the rope with all his strength. Both hind-legs were snapped up, the defiant head was jerked back, and in a high, aerial somersault the moss-head was busted, hard. He was up again, struggling, and Mace busted him again. The third time he lay there and Bowman went down the rope to tie him in less than eight minutes.

Such a battle of rider and steer had never been seen in the arena of Pioneer Park and the crowd gave a mighty cheer; but Brown Jug was puffing and lathering with sweat as he turned back towards the chutes. Only one steer tied down, and horse and rider were showing the strain when McMullen looked them over at the scratch.

"Eh, hey!" he laughed. "*Only* nine more—look at this one!" And he jerked his thumb towards the corral.

A long, agile black creature came humping out the chutes, throwing kinks in his back as he looked to right and left for some man or horse to fight. He was an imported steer from the mesquite thickets of Central Texas and when he sighted Bowman he charged. Judges and starters fled right and left as the wicked white horns flashed in the sun. But Brown Jug dodged him nimbly and when the dust cleared away Mace had snared him around the neck.

He threw the slack behind his legs, took a quick run to the left and busted the black steer on his back. But there was a pop, a loud report, as he hit the ground, and Mace reached for his other rope. His manila whale-line had parted and the steer, leaping up, tossed his head and blatted with rage. Then he charged and, while he tied his spare rope to the horn, Bowman took ignominiously to flight.

Brown Jug snorted and shied as with ears pointed

ahcad he faced the brandishing horns. He doubled and turned again and as they dashed past the stands the Hash-knife boys whooped with joy. But Long Rope's blood was up and when he had built his loop he whipped in and tied to the brute. They went into a tangle of darting legs and flashing horns and Bowman busted him again, but each time he hit the ground the black steer bounced up and charged back into the fight. Then Jug stepped on the rope as he was leaping away and one long, polished horn found its mark. With a squeal Brown Jug kicked, circled frantically to the left while his master handled the slack; but at the yank his hurt leg weakened and he went down on his side, just as Mace leapt off to tie. For the steer was down too, and before he could struggle up Bowman had him by the hind leg. Without it under him the brutc could not rise and Long Rope fought him down on his side. Then he grabbed the two front-feet, cast his loop around them and caught one hind-foot in the slack. With all the strength of his brawny shoulders he drew the three legs together, took his dallies and tied the steer fast. But when he threw up his hands for the judges he saw that Brown Jug was hurt.

He lay tangled in the rope, his eyes rolling wildly, blood flowing from a deep hole in his leg. Stout-hearted Little Jug, he had fought to the end, but the pace had been too swift! Bowman knelt down beside him, ramming his handkerchief into the hole to quench the first gush of blood, and as a doctor came running they bound the wound up tight and Jug rose to his feet with a grunt.

"Poor old Jug!" muttered Mace, almost in tears as he led him off; and a silence fell on the crowd. But as they passed the corrals a mocking voice saluted them.

"Eh, hey! And *only* eight more!"

"Don't you worry!" yelled back Bowman in a fury. "I'll tie 'em, just to see you get killed!"

"Even money on McMullen!" offered a sport in the stands. But no one took him up. The goring of Brown Jug had sobered the Bowman partisans, and as suddenly the Hash-knives took heart.

"Two to one!" they shouted. "Three to one on Tex!"

But all the Bowman money had disappeared. Men who had walked the streets the night before offering two to one on Mace sat stunned and silenced by the disaster. All they had thought about then was the ferocity of Matador, a stag from the bull-rings of Mexico; but now they perceived that the ten Hash-knife steers were in the man-killing class themselves. The first had put up a battle, the second had gored Mace's horse—the third or the tenth might kill him.

"Ten to one!" shouted Colonel Jones, waving his roll exultantly. "Five thousand that McMullen wins!"

Then the tall, slender figure of James G. Cramer rose up and nodded an affable acceptance.

"Taken!" he said, making his way through the crowd. "And I'll lay you five thousand more."

"Very well!" agreed the showman, "if you'll accept my check."

"Anyone else?" inquired Cramer, looking about.

"Five to one!" offered a sporting man, reneging; but

the barkeeper did not mind the odds. He was writing out slips like a bookmaker with the odds back to two to one, when from the mysterious corral in which he kept his mounts Mace Bowman came riding forth. Brown Jug had been put out of the running, but in his place he was riding Scrambled Eggs!

A gasp came from the crowd as they recognized the golden coat of the swift-stepping, redoubtable Eggs—the champion rope-horse of the world! Then a quick-thinking sport shot his hand into the air and flourished a huge roll of bills.

"Even money on Long Rope!" he announced; but the rest of the audience sat dumb.

Mace rode out easily, lolling back in the saddle with one hand on Scrambled Egg's rump. He bowed, doffing his hat in imitation of McMullen, and Colonel Jones sprang up, cursing. Then, with all eyes upon him, Mace lifted his hand and they saw the big Hash-knife on Eggs' hip. But, burned above and below in two-inch letters, was the legend MEALS 25 CENTS!

Jones slumped back in his seat, for the public scorn of his penury had at last got under his hide, and the mountain-men let out a roar. Bowman rode grimly past and through the small gate that led to the inner field. His slight at the Hash-knife wagon had been repaid.

He had Eggs on the scratch, rope up to make his start, when Tex McMullen came galloping towards him.

"I protest!" he yelled to the judges. "He's riding my

top rope-hawse! There's some monkey-business—Scrambled Eggs was stole!"

"No, he wasn't!" answered Mace. "He was sold—by Colonel Jones—and here's my bill of sale!"

He drew a paper from his pocket and after a hasty conference the judges motioned McMullen away. The field was cleared, the flagmen set, and as another great steer charged forth Bowman shot out after him and passed him like a flash. Scrambled Eggs was in his glory, rejoicing in his speed and the old game he knew so well; and as Long Rope tied to the steer, Eggs went to the end of the rope and snapped him off his feet. The steer rose groggily, Mace whirled and scampered off again; and the wild terror of the hills, as his head was jerked beneath him, hit the earth with a resounding thump. Long Rope went down his twine for the record time of the day and the cowboys in the grandstand whooped.

"Send 'em out!" ordered Mace, riding back to the chutes; and in less than ten minutes he had tied two more steers, for Eggs was at his best. He stood dancing behind the mark, then he shot across the line like a wolfhound after a goat; and when he felt the rope tighten and his master reined away he hit the rope with all his strength. Mace rose up laughing as he made the last swift tie and turned to where McMullen sat his horse.

"Eh, hey!" he taunted. "And *only* five more!"

But now there was a tumult in the crowd.

"Bring out Matador!" they clamored in a chorus. "Let Mace rest—we want Matador!"

They had come there for combat and blood on the sands, but Bowman had the contest in his hands. They knew that he could tie his five steers in jig-time and they turned as one man on Tex.

"Let Bowman tie his ten first!" he yapped back, as Red Tutlow, the Arena Director, called him out. "That's the agreement we made and I'm standing on my rights. You're trying to git me killed!"

"No, I'm not," denied Red, "but can't you hear 'em yell? They want you to rope Matador."

"To hell with 'em!" scoffed Tex. "I'm not gitting myself busted to give them hey-rubes a laugh. And Bowman can't claim that prize money until he ties down every steer."

"Well, turn 'em out!" spoke up Mace. "I'm ready and waiting."

But the crowd was vehement in its protests. They stamped their feet and shouted, swarming down over the railing to call Tex a coward to his face; until at last, though reluctantly, he gave in.

"But, mind you, this don't count!" he warned. "You've called me out of my turn. If I fail to tie him now I claim the right to try again, after he's tied down his other five."

"All right!" agreed Mace.

"All right!" agreed the judges. And the crowd climbed back into the stands.

Bowman could see the crafty game that McMullen was playing. He had turned the public clamor to good account, for now he had a chance to try out Matador without having the time count against him. It was a "Heads I win, tails you lose" proposition as far as Tex was concerned, but Long Rope knew Matador. He knew that no man living, with a thirty-foot rope, could tie him without getting killed. And ever since the Texan had mocked at Brown Jug's hurts, Mace had had but one thought—revenge!

He leaned back, smiling confidently, as Tex mounted his Roman-nosed black and shook out his puny loop. They had laughed at Mace, and at the great bundle of manila rope that had given him his name of Long Rope—which was another name for a cow-thief. Perhaps, as they had said, he had stolen some widow-woman's clothesline; and then again perhaps, when it came to longhorned steers, fifty feet was none too much.

Seeing McMullen with his short contest rope it came over Mace that he had had no real intention of competing. He and his Hash-knife backers had planned to buy such murderous steers that no man in the world could tie them. They had hoped to get him busted—maimed or killed as the case might be—and win the purse by default. For unless Bowman finished his full ten, McMullen was not obligated to compete. But the clamor of the populace had disrupted their well-laid plans and Tex was up against the prod.

"All right!" he called at last, and the stock-car door was pulled open. There was a long, expectant pause, but Matador did not appear. He hung back in the dark interior, a dim black form with horns that whacked against the walls. Then at a jab from behind he edged them out through the doorway and McMullen reined back his horse.

Matador too was black, like the steer that had gored Brown Jug, and his horns had a long double curve. They grew straight out from his head, turned forward and up, then straightened out in sharp, black-tipped points. But what shoulders he had, and what quick-stepping hind-legs, like the quarters of a Spanish bull! For Matador was a stag, built high to bear his horns, but lacking nothing of his bull-ring speed. And what horns—at least seven feet across—as long as his huge-muscled body!

Every horseman in the arena reined back as he vaulted out, taking shelter behind the rows of posts, and as Bowman looked at Tex he could see his eyes grow big. He was scared stiff—afraid to start! Matador smelled the ground as he felt it beneath his feet, shaking his head with a high, anguished *mmwoo;* and as he stood with his feet braced as if against a fall, Mace saw that his eyes were stone-white. After a week in the darkness of the car the sudden burst of sunlight had blinded him. He was helpless and McMullen seized his chance.

With a thunder of feet the big black crossed the mark, Tex built half his rope into a loop; but as Roman-nose galloped in, the stag heard him coming and thrust out one horn like a lance. Then he bellowed, pawing the earth as he lurched towards the sound, and the horse broke his stride and shied.

McMullen lashed out with his loop, but the horse had spoiled his throw and the next instant Matador charged. There was a tangle of flying rope and black bodies in the dust, flashing legs and quick, dodging turns; and then from the maelstrom the startled horse shot forth with a long horn close at his heels.

But Matador stopped short, turning the whites of his blinded eyes to the sun, and McMullen edged in again. Every rider in the field had ducked out of sight, each thinking of the safety of his mount; and now in the sudden quiet they crowded into the corrals and climbed up on the fence to look. Tex was spurring in closer, taking desperate chances to jerk down the stag while he was blind; and from grandstand and fence alike his friends roared advice and encouragement. Thousands of dollars were up, partisan feeling was at white-heat, and with the shouts of advice there blended derisive whoops; but Tex ignored them all. He was watching intently, to make sure the steer was blind. Then he whirled his wide loop and charged.

Bowman almost said his prayers as he beheld Matador at the mercy of his hated foe. After all his efforts to bring him up from Mexico the hot sun had seared his eyeballs. He was helpless—and Tex made his throw. The loop circled the wide horns and, without waiting to jerk it taut, McMullen jumped his horse to the left. But as the rope yanked at his neck Matador let out a roar and went with it, straight at the horse. The ground trembled when they struck and went down together, and above the whirl of dust Mace could see Tex McMullen, struggling desperately to throw off his rope. Then he shot out through the air and landed on the run, leaving his horse at the mercy of the steer.

There was bawling and squealing, the heart-stilling sound of kicks and heavy falls; then a loud, resonant pop as the stout grass-rope parted and the horse clattered across the park. Matador heaved up, rolling his eyes as he stared about, and suddenly the wild clamor ceased.

"I pass!" shouted McMullen from the top of the fence. For at last the man-killer could see.

CHAPTER XXIX
THE THOUSAND DOLLAR BILL

THE Contest of the Century came to an end precipitately when Matador got back his sight, and he put on a show of his own. He bucked and bawled, pawing up the dirt like a bull and circling around the field; and then, when McMullen tried to sneak out his mount, he chased him over the fence. Others toled the horse away and got him into the corral, though somewhat the worst for wear; and when the fighting steer was trapped in the bronk-pen the match was called off for the day.

The crowd trooped back to town, well satisfied with the announcement that the contest would be settled in the morning; for they had received their full money's worth of bloodshed and excitement, and neither side had won. Tex McMullen had passed, but he had refuted the charge that he was yellow and afraid of Matador. He had tied to him twice and, but for the shortness of his rope, he might easily have won the crown. But now that the huge stag had recovered his sight it was even money that Tex was through. He laughed off his defeat, which had cost him nothing but the experience, and went into conference with his backers, and that night in the back room of the Long Horn Saloon the Committee of Three took counsel.

Mace had sprung a surprise on the unsuspecting Hash-knives when he had ridden out on Scrambled Eggs, and if all went well in the morning he would win the contest, hands down. But since McMullen had had his chance and had failed to tie Matador, his backers would seek some other way out. Already there were rumors on the street that Scrambled Eggs would be replevined by the Colonel on the ground that he had been obtained by fraud—anything to tie him up and keep Bowman from having the use of him. But Mace still had an ace in the hole.

"All I ask of you fellows," he said, "is that you keep watch over Matador. I'm going to take Eggs and spend the night out on the desert, where even the coyotes can't find me. And when I come back—hold your breath! I'll be leading Whistling Rufus!"

"That's the stuff!" applauded Tutlow. "But can you work him against these steers?"

"He'll be mighty wild and snuffy," admitted Mace.

"But there's one thing—he ain't afraid! He'd walk right up to old Matador and never bat an eye. But when the Hash-knives see that I've got another rope-horse, McMullen will up and quit. He'd better, or Matador will kill him."

"Well, we don't want that," spoke up Cramer, "because of course this is a sporting event. But with all that money up, and his own prestige at stake, Colonel Jones will *make* him rope. I've heard repeatedly that Tex blames his short rope for his failure to tie Matador—"

"He was scared!" broke in Bowman, "and that's all there is to it. I don't give a dam' what happens to him. He mighty near laughed his head off when poor old Jug got gored—now I want to see him tie *my* steer."

There was a rap at the door and Phat Noland slipped in.

"Sowbelly Johnson is out there," he said, "and he wants to see you, Mace. He's drunk as a goat and says it's very important. And he's got two important drunk friends."

"Hash-knife men?" inquired Bowman cautiously.

"Nope—out-of-town sports. Flashing quite a little money. They won't take 'No' for an answer."

"Just a minute!" broke in Cramer as Long Rope rose to go. "We can't be too careful, tonight. Red, you go out and look these friends over. And Mace, you stay right here."

"All right," agreed Mace, settling back, "old Sowbelly is no friend of mine. The doggoned old tarrapin, it sure hurt his pride when I beat the wagon out of two-bits."

"You go along too, Phat," directed Cramer, "and scout down the street for the Hash-knives. And tell Mr. Johnson that Mace is in conference with his manager."

He leaned back and sighed as he met Bowman's eyes.

"I sometimes wonder," he said, "whether the game is worth the candle. Whether my dream of a North America without Irish policemen is anything more than a Utopia. These enemies we have made are in a desperate mood tonight. They're going to get you, if they can."

"Let 'em try!" answered Mace. "I'll take 'em all on. Maybe after I beat Tex and we nick the Colonel again they'll learn to leave us alone."

"Not as long as the Gulf Stream warms the cold bosom of Ireland, and I fear we will never divert it. But what about Eva, my boy? Do you remember the message you left?"

"Sure do," returned Bowman expectantly. "What did she say—or did you see her?"

"You said," went on the barkeeper dreamily, "that you'd never forget that kiss. And if she ever kissed you again like that you were going to run away with her. When I repeated those words she almost hugged me, for of course she's only a child, and then she laughed to herself.

"'He's always making jokes,' she said. 'Do you think he actually would?'

" 'I do!' I answered. 'He's a boy of great spirit.'

" 'Well, tell him to look out, then,' she said. And with that she skipped away."

"When was this?" asked Mace at last. "Last fall, when she went back East?"

"The very day she left! And her mother was angry because she ran back to speak to a barkeep!"

"Aw—her!" scoffed Bowman. "She can't bear to speak to anybody. I met her yesterday, and the look she gave me would cut your heart in two. They must have changed Little Eva in the cradle, because the first time I see her we was friends. I wonder what she meant by that, now—when she told you I'd better look out!"

"It's my guess," opined Cramer, "that Eva is coming back. And when she does come she's going to kiss you and see if you'll take a dare!"

"Ump-umm!" decided Mace, after a long, thoughtful pause. "She'd never kiss me, now. But by the gods, if she does—"

"That's the talk!" nodded the barkeep, approvingly. "Be a man or a mouse—and if Merry Hart butts in, you tell her that Eva is eighteen!"

"Yes, but is she?" challenged Bowman.

"The day before yesterday was her birthday," answered Cramer. "I know, because she wrote me a letter."

"Aha!" spoke up Mace, his eyes brightening. But before he could ask what she said there was a thunderous knock on the door.

"Come out of there!" rumbled a voice, "and settle a bet for us!" And when they looked out it was Satchel Vest Steen.

"Aw, go off and die!" came back Long Rope. "What do I care about you and your bets?"

"It ain't me," defended Steen. "It's Sowbelly Johnson. Come on, it won't take a minute."

"All right," agreed Mace, after a doubtful glance at Cramer; and they went out into the barroom.

It was crammed to the doors with an ever-shifting crowd; and up against the bar, with two strangers beside him, stood Sowbelly Johnson, drunk.

"Thar he is!" he declaimed as Long Rope came in. "You're my friend, now ain't you, Mace? Old-time friends—used to swamp for me with the Diamond As. Say, Mace, do you remember that time when you come back, when I was cooking for the Hash-knife wagon? Stingiest outfit I ever worked for—made me charge for meals. Remember how I gave you a meal?"

"Oh, sure!" grinned Bowman, trying to humor him. "And a danged good meal, Mr. Johnson."

"Now—you see?" crowed Sowbelly, turning to look at the two strangers. "These gentlemen thought I was lying. Seeing that brand on Scrambled Eggs is what brought it up. MEALS 25 CENTS—eh, Mace? Well, I told 'em after you et you offered a thousand dollar bill—and I didn't have the *change!*"

He burst out laughing and slapped Bowman on the back.

"You recollect that—don't you, Mace?"

"W'y sure!" responded Long Rope heartily. "That was a horse on the Colonel, wasn't it?"

"Well, we got into an argument—and Mort Steen joined in—and I bet every dollar I've got in the world that you did have a thousand dollar bill. You had it, and you offered it, and I couldn't make the change. Now, that's right, ain't it, Mace? To decide a bet!"

"Well, I say he did *not!*" broke in Satchel Vest. "He might have flashed a bill and *said* it was a grand—"

"Now, wait!" protested one of the strangers. "Just leave it to Mr. Bowman to decide."

"Aw, bull!" scoffed Steen. "That guy will tell you anything! He never had no thousand dollar bill. I know that old stall of putting your thumb over a ten—"

"Oh! I didn't, eh?" came back Mace, reaching down into his boot. "Just cast your eye on that, old horse!"

A sharp elbow dug into his ribs as he rose up with the bill and Red Tutlow faced him, scowling. Then a long, hairy arm reached over his shoulder and snatched half the bill away.

"You can't get away with that!" croaked a voice from behind, and as he whirled he beheld Gilhooly. There was a triumphant grin on his bearded lips, but just as he ducked away Bowman smashed him on the jaw. Then an avalanche of men seemed to fall on him, and as he went down he felt the handcuffs nip his wrists.

"You're under arrest," announced one of the drunk strangers, who had suddenly shed his jag. "I'll hold this bill as evidence."

He wrenched the torn bill from Mace's clenched fist and looked it over curiously. Then he leaned over Gilhooly, who had taken the count, and removed the other half from his paw.

"Well!" challenged Bowman, as he saw his face change. "What's the charge, Mr. Man—what's the charge?"

"Possessing counterfeit money," responded the Federal agent. "But—er—this bill seems perfectly good."

"It ought to be," came back Mace. "I got it from Neil Monroe, and he's president of the First National Bank. So take off these nippers—and next time you make a pinch be a little more choice of your friends."

He glanced contemptuously at Sowbelly, booted Gilhooly out of the road, and snatched back the torn halves of his bill.

"I've been looking for this for nigh onto a year," he said. And as he ducked out the door he laughed.

CHAPTER XXX "WHOOPEELAH!"

BEFORE the crowded grandstand when morning came the two Champions rode forth to do battle, but each man had changed his front. On the first day McMullen had led the way, bowing regally to his admirers as they cheered; but now he hung back, for the gods had turned against him, and Long Rope took the lead. On his head like a crown he wore the white beaver sombrero which he had won the year before from Tex, and in place of his blue jumper he had on McMullen's shirt—cloth-of-gold with the purple *fleur-de-lis* of France. His boots were polished, his silver champion-plate all a-gleam; and he was mounted on high-headed Scrambled Eggs, now christened MEALS TWENTY FIVE CENTS.

Mace rode back and forth up the empty track, nodding and smiling, waving his hand; and from time to time as he halted before the stands his eyes scanned the faces above. All the youth and beauty of El Toro was present, and many fair faces that were strange; but nowhere among them could he spy Little Eva, though something in the words of James G. Cramer had roused a new hope in his breast. But now he was called upon to rope.

"Turn him out!" he said as he stood Meals behind the line and held up his loop for the start. "Turn him out and we'll bust him—me and Meals Twenty-five Cents—the finest little rope-horse in the world!"

He patted Meals's neck as the steer came ramping from the chute, and when he crossed the line Meals charged out fearlessly while Mace whirled his loop for the throw. He noosed both horns and turned abruptly to the left and, the gods so ordaining, they caught the steer off the ground and stood him on his head. One moment he was running, head high and on the prod; the next he was yanked through the air like a kite and piled up in a heap. Mace went down his rope the instant the steer hit and grappled him by the hind-foot. Then with knee and shoulders he drew three legs together and tied them hard and fast.

The crowd cheered, and Bowman bowed, and when the next steer came out he flashed in and did it again.

"Eh, hey!" he hollered, turning to grin at McMullen, "*only* three more! Whoopeelah!"

He danced a kind of jig in his stirrups while Meals pranced and shook his head, and they tied another one down. The last two came harder, but Mace and Meals were going strong and, willy-nilly, they laid them out. Then, with his last tie made, Long Rope rode back in triumph while the announcer bellowed his time. it had taken more than forty-two minutes for him to rope and tie his ten steers; and now it was up to McMullen to tie down Matador in less. Twist and scheme as they would the Hash-knife backers had failed to stave off the final test; and now, all talking at once, they crowded around Tex, whose face was working angrily.

"No!" he shouted back. "I'm not going to rope. Do you think I want to git killed?"

"You can do it!" thundered Satchel Vest. "Think of the money we've got up! Go on in and try—you've got forty-two minutes."

But McMullen shook his head.

"I tied to him yesterday," he said. "And once is enough, for me. The man don't live that can tie that brute down—I don't care what you say."

"All right!" spoke up Bowman. "I claim the match, then. I'm the Champion Steer Roper of the World."

"Oh, you are, eh?" came back Tex. "Well, *you* go in and tie him!"

"Ump-umm!" laughed Mace. "That wasn't the agreement. I got him for you to tie."

"You got him to kill me!" accused McMullen. "Look at all the Mexicans he gored!"

"Yes, and look at them ten steers that you sawed off on me. You was trying to get *me* killed. You never had no intention of roping Matador. You're yaller, you pot-licking hound!"

He spurred in closer and looked Tex in the eye, and with a curse McMullen snatched up his rope.

"I'll show you!" he gritted. "You dadburned whelp, you cain't claim no decision over me. I'll go in and bust him if I git killed doing it. And then I reckon you'll *laugh!*"

"That's what you did," answered Mace, "when my horse got gored. Go in and try some of it yourself!"

"Ahrr!" snarled Tex and, ignoring the cheering crowd, he rode in to face Matador. But now, instead of his short maguey throw-rope, he held a huge coil of whale-line in his hand; and in place of the Roman-nosed black he was mounted on a broad-rumped bay.

"Turn him out!" he shouted as he took his stand at the bronk-corral where Matador had been penned overnight; and as the chute was thrown open a great silence fell and every man in the arena climbed the fence. There was a rattle of prod-poles as the corral-men punched and jabbed and then, bellowing savagely, the great steer burst forth and stood in the open at gaze.

"Mm-woo-woo!" he complained, tossing his head;

and at sight of a flagman in the distance he set out in a long, purposeful trot. He held his spreading horns high, spurning the ground with angry feet, and his bulging eyes burned like fire. But as he lined out down the field Tex McMullen galloped after him, swinging his loop and rising for the throw. He was spurring in desperately when Matador stopped short and faced about with an angry snort.

"Baw!" he bawled and before Tex could turn he lowered his horns and charged. His long, lance-like horn had almost reached the startled bay when he squatted and leapt to the left, but in the middle of the bolt McMullen lashed back with his rope and the loop settled over one horn. The bay plunged to one side to jerk the steer down—but Tex had forgotten his long rope. He set himself for the yank but it trailed out endlessly, and by the time the fifty feet of slack was taken up Matador had shaken off the loop. Shaken it off and charged again, and at the angry blat behind him the bay almost jumped out of his skin. Then he ran, snorting with terror, while close at his heels the long, wicked horns bowed and hooked.

McMullen turned in his saddle to build another loop, but as coil after coil piled up in his left hand he threw the rope down in a pet. He was a short-rope man and the long piece of whale-line had lost him what chance he had. The bay twisted and turned, almost throwing his rider as he dodged the whirlwind charges; and then, running frantically, he stepped on the dragging rope and they all went down in a heap.

There was a shout from the grandstand as the dust swirled up and McMullen emerged from the ruck. He was running for the fence and, closer and closer behind, Matador came with romping leaps. His black tail lashed back and forth, his horns hooked the empty air; but just as he plunged in to strike down his victim McMullen seemed to rise up and fly. He ran the fastest race of his life and missed sudden death by a hair.

"My Gawd!" he gasped as he tottered back to the judges' stand. "Did you see him hook my shirt? How the hell I got away without being killed is more than I can tell. He's the outfightingest brute in the world!"

"So you quit, eh?" spoke up Mace.

"Yes, I quit!" quavered Tex. "And there ain't a man on earth that can rope and tie that steer."

"All right, then," said Long Rope. "I claim the purse and bet, and the Championship of the World. And it sure done me good to see you outrun that steer. I knowed you could do it if you tried."

He slapped his leg and laughed and McMullen burst out cursing.

"I've said it before," he wailed, "and I'll say it again. You're a good skater all summer and a good swimmer all winter. I dare you to rope that steer!"

"Well, dare all you want to," answered Mace. "I've won enough money to buy me a nice bunch of cows. I don't have to rope that steer!"

"You're afraid to!" yapped McMullen, following after him as he went to his horse, and the Hash-knife crowd joined in. They were all in an angry mood, for they had lost a lot of money, and while they clamored Colonel Jones strode in.

"I'll bet you ten to one you can't tie that steer," he challenged. "Up to any amount you name!"

"Don't you do it!" yelled Cramer and Tutlow as they saw Mace's eyes light up. But the baiting had gone too far.

"I'll go you!" he said, "for ten thousand dollars!" And he rode out to his guarded corral.

Matador was still bellowing and pawing up the earth when the Champion of the World rode back, but now instead of Meals he bestrode such a rampant steed that the crowd rushed back into the stands. There was a high, snorting whistle, as with mane and tail afloat Whistling Rufus came sidewinding down the track, his great eyes burning like fire. He wheeled and shied again as the audience rose to look, but at the touch of his rider's spurs he went bucking and plunging towards the gate.

He was almost out of his head from fear and excitement, but when he darted through the opening and came face-to-face with Matador he halted and arched his neck. Here was something he knew, a wild steer off the plains, pawing the earth in a challenge to battle. Rufus drew a great breath and snorted back defiance, while Bowman shook out his loop. He reined off to the left, circling around the savage beast, swinging his rope and waiting for the throw. But Matador, drooling froth, stood sullenly at bay, his feet deep in the hole they had dug.

Long Rope wheeled and galloped off, trying to draw him in pursuit, but the wild steer had sensed the invincible spirit of Whistling Rufus and he lowered his head and roared. The earth seemed to tremble beneath that deep, muffled rumbling so potent with menace and blood lust, and from the grandstands the screams of women stabbed through it in stark terror, for death was in the air. Here was no contest of man and horse against a steer, but a battle for life itself. Even Bowman kept his distance, for he had seen the lightning charge by which the steer struck down his foes. But Rufus shook out his mane and, holding his arched head low, trotted arrogantly in on the beast.

"Go get 'im, boy!" exulted Mace as he felt the battling spirit of this champion of the plains; and while the crowd looked on in awe, Rufus whistled a challenge and charged. But Matador had lost the devastating rage that had impelled him to impetuous attack, and as the horse raced by he stood fast, brandishing his horns and pawing up dust. Bowman shook out a wider loop and turned back at him purposefully, and with a snort the great steer fled. The stands were in a furore as Mace rose to make his throw, and as the noose fell true they gave a roar, but before he could jerk the loop taut the steer leapt through it and sped away.

Long Rope had done his best but the spread of those mighty horns had defied his greatest skill. Any loop that would encircle them would let the steer himself pass through—his horns were longer than his body.

Mace reined away to think it over while he built another loop and the steer took courage and stopped. Then he came back, brandishing his head and bellowing, and Rufus circled away. He knew from many battles with outlaw bulls which end to hold in fear, and as Matador plunged in he eluded his rush and sprang after him as he passed.

There was a gleam of snapping teeth, the piston-like stroke of hoofs; but as the huge head swung back Whistling Rufus darted away, and once more Mace slapped on his loop. They were lost in a cloud of dust as steer and horse whirled and fought, but with a jerk and a jab of spurs Bowman broke up the fight and jumped his precious mount out of reach. One blow from those twisted horns and glorious Whistling Rufus would be stretched out dead on the field. It was not worth the price—and yet it hurt Bowman's pride to fail with such a horse. McMullen's terrified mounts had spoiled every throw, thinking of nothing but to escape being gored; but here was a mustang that would match his teeth and hoofs against the fiercest bull on the plains.

Mace built a smaller loop and rode in on Matador, trying to start him once more to flight. For, though his horns were broad, there was another way yet of getting a rope on his neck. The steer stood at bay, mooing complainingly as he pawed the earth, and Bowman circled him warily. Then as he stirred up a cloud of dust he jumped Rufus through it and lashed the steer on the rump. Again and again he whipped in and out, laying the rope on Matador's hide; until at last, bellowing angrily, he lined out down the field, with Whistling Rufus close behind. Bowman came up on the run, swinging his shortened loop and watching each stroke of his feet; then as the steer left the ground he whipped the noose under all four feet and jerked it taut around his neck!

There was a cheer that split the air as the crowd beheld Matador roped, but without a moment's pause Mace threw his slack to the right and gave Whistling Rufus the spurs. They went past like a shot, man and horse leaning forward vengefully as the steer still galloped on; and then like a bombshell he exploded in mid-air and came down with a devastating smash. One horn snapped short off, the tangled body went end for end and Bowman dropped off in the dust. He grabbed at a limp hind-leg, reaching forward with his tie-string and snaring the two front-feet. Then with a triumphant jerk he yanked all three together and tied them hard and fast. It was not until the judges came out that he noticed that the steer's neck was broke.

Whistling Rufus was still snorting and fighting his head when Long Rope rode him back to the stands, but Bowman himself was tired. He had won the Hashknives' money and bested Tex McMullen, but the cheers of the populace meant nothing. If it had happened the other way they would be shouting for Tex, and Mace was not a show-hand. He sat his horse dumbly until the clamor died down and Colonel Jones left his box in a huff. Then he patted Rufus on the neck and was reining away when a clear voice called his name.

"Hello, Túcumcari!" it hailed; and, stopping short, he looked back at the stands.

They were thinning out now, but somewhere in that crowd a woman had called his name.

"Whoopeelah!" she cried; and, far up towards the top, he saw a waving hand. It was Little Eva—his girl!

He straightened up with a start as he beheld her smiling face where before all had been a void. Then, taking down his rope, he built a quick loop and flipped it over the end of a rafter. He jerked the loop tight, leapt up on Rufus's back, and swung himself out through space —high over the heads of the people until he landed in the stands beside Eva. She was taller by two inches, and prettier than ever, for there was a love light in her smiling blue eyes.

"How's my girl?" he asked, clasping her hands; but Eva seemed to expect something more.

"*My* girl!" he repeated, picking her up and kissing her; and the crowd burst into a cheer.

"I *told* you to look out!" she laughed; and kissed him in the sight of them all. Then they stepped up on Whistling Rufus, who bucked, and rode off to make good their word. For a promise is a promise, and Little Eva had kissed him just as sweetly as she had before.